Stones

Novels by Dennis Bowen

THE WATER DIAMONDS
Book 1: International Thriller Series

THE BLACKSTONE PERFECTION
Book 2: International Thriller Series

THE CRYSTAL SEDUCTION
Book 3: International Thriller Series

THE REDROCK QUARANTINE
Book 4: International Thriller Series

THE FINAL MASQUERADE
Book 5: International Thriller Series

Stones

Dennis Bowen

ISBN: 978-0-9979147-5-7

FIRST EDITION

www.DennisBowen.com

www.twitter.com/DBowenThrillers

www.facebook.com/DennisBowenThrillers

Book Interior Design by 52 Novels

ACKNOWLEDGMENTS

Thank you to the readers who have immersed themselves in my *International Thriller Series*. While I create the intrigues that span the globe and enjoy every minute of it, in the end, I write these novels for you and your enjoyment. It's that simple.

As with *The Water Diamonds*, *The Blackstone Perfection*, *The Crystal Seduction*, *The Redrock Quarantine*, and *The Final Masquerade*, those who offered suggestions and encouragement during the writing of *Stones* deserve my appreciation.

I once again express my appreciation to Laura Taylor. Her editorial consultations have kept my manuscripts clean and tight. As in life, each successive endeavor—such as writing a series of novels—is built on what came before. Laura has provided just the right touch—a hand neither too heavy nor too light—in order that each novel is correct in presentation while preserving what I as a novelist have brought to the table. As before, any errors or omissions in *Stones*, I claim as my own.

I extend my gratitude to family members and friends for their support, and to former colleagues, some of whom offered up their lives in the service of this great country, and whose presence in my life gives my stories their noted sense of reality. Thank you to all.

—Dennis Bowen

To the Reader

It is not uncommon within the intelligence community to meet or work with someone who gives a false name, whose employer and job title are likewise untrue, and who may actually be in the employ of your lethal enemy.

My stories, as experienced in the companion *International Thriller Series*, are intended to portray to each reader those severe and potentially lethal risks and exposures. Yet, as in the rest of life, there is always the humanity. The caring of participants for one another sometimes results in unfounded, catastrophic trust, and even love itself.

I write these stories for those of us, domestic and foreign, who have spent time in a world where reality and fiction coincide in the same space and time, and for those who have not.

I hope you enjoy reading my tales of global intrigues, espionage, and the inevitable conflicts that continue to play out in the actual world and show no signs of abating.

May peace someday come to all who deserve life, liberty, and the pursuit of happiness. Such deserves to be the end product of all those who engage evil at great risk to themselves, but who wouldn't have it any other way.

—*Dennis Bowen*

PROLOGUE

Frostbite."

"Another . . . step."

"Just . . . another . . . step."

Breathless words escaped near frozen lips.

No signal of pain transmitted up his legs. He could not feel them at all. His home on the American eastern seaboard experienced low temperatures. This was Maryland cold times five. He'd heard that Soviet political prisoners had been sent to prisons in realms like this. Their sentences proved immaterial. They lasted three weeks.

"Do I . . . care?"

"No."

"Not . . . now."

That his mind chose the least of all evils was a tell. It was shutting down. Giving up. He purged the notion of frostbite from his universe.

He needed to run. The hostile environment turned his attempt into a trudge. The wetness and depth of the new snow sucked his hi-tech snowshoes from his feet.

The noises behind. The dogs. Their masters.

His every breath frosted into the whiteout surround.

He twisted his head. The blur of lights.

Sounds propagated in the wet air. The whir of combat snowmobiles and the trundle of snowcats surrounded him. His enemies—everywhere. Seventy soldiers, at least, in the hunt.

He turned, his GPS ear-buds guiding him back toward the frozen channel.

There. He started down a bank. Onto the ice-bridge.

Two-point-four miles to land. To the other island. Half of that to political safety. All of it to physical safety.

Random bullets of frustrated pursuers. Some poofed into the snow nearby, others buzzed his head. After pursuing the red flesh he'd left to the south of the Russian fortress as bait, the dogs had recovered. And the sequenced flares he'd positioned to distract heat sensors. Burned out.

In perfect shape prior to his exile, he'd added winter insulation for the operation—like the native population. Like the Inupiat.

He slowed.

He tired.

There!

With white in every direction, his GPS watch propelled him onward … just ahead … he struggled … ten more steps …

The man, early thirties, six feet tall, fell forward onto crusted snow.

He pushed up. Onto exhausted legs. He pressed on.

The pulsing bark of AK-47's grew louder now. His pursuers, themselves exiled to their country's nether region due to some presumed infractions, possessed no hi-tech visual devices. They employed dated methods. Their tracking animals, senses diminished by temperatures far below freezing, slowly acquired the scent of the red drops behind him that punctuated the white blanket.

He dared not stop. Not even to catch a breath. The inter-island bridge, created of ice in the dead of winter, could collapse.

Abruptly.

Any breach in its structure would dump him from sight into a fluid of death—the forbidding Bering Sea.

"It . . . should . . . never . . . be . . . this . . . cold," he gasped between breaths.

His boots sucked his legs into the deep snow as he lurched forward.

"Never . . . this . . . cold."

The mantra helped.

Three more bullets bore through the blizzard, their report drowned out by the howl of nature. Of the gale-force winds.

East. He pushed east. An eyes-up display inside his hi-tech goggles confirmed.

More bullets, courtesy of the Russian security units behind.

In desperation, he gulped the frozen air that blew off the Siberian coast. It burned without warmth.

Sounds, now much closer, speared the whiteout.

Dogs. Trained to take down, not kill, would catch him. Preserve him for an interrogation no god could countenance. The fugitive preferred death. Without it, he would be captured. There would be no trial. He would non-exist.

A lull in the wind.

His mind numbed, he stabbed at the mantra. "Never . . . this . . . cold."

A break in the white ahead. He trudged. "Low risk," he'd been told. The op was low risk. Andrew Scott had lied.

Hypothermia. His mind numbed further. For a second, he thought he saw a figure ahead.

A sound barely escaped his lips. "Help!"

At that moment, his body pitched forward, planting in the deep powder.

The dogs, and their handlers, were almost upon him.

It was over. Best to die.

The last words he heard before he passed out... "You have crossed the International Date Line. You are now entering the United States of America. Welcome. Valid passport required."

The welcome was repeated in Russian.

• • •

"*Da!* This way." The major led his men toward the end of Russia—toward what the Americans called freedom.

"Press on!"

After fifteen more feet, he turned.

Exhausted, his men hadn't moved.

"We are at the last eastern outpost, because we are the Russian equivalent of the French Foreign Legion. If we fail, there is only one punishment available. *Khorosho?*"

"Da!" those few who could hear him cried out in staccato fashion.

• • •

A bolt of lightning and the whiteout-surround played the biblical flash of white light. Strong arms pulling him awakened the fallen operative for a precious moment, as if to deliver him to the hereafter.

Not enough.

The white cloud of swirling snow abated. Faded. To black.

• • •

The strong arms were real. They hefted the near-dead operative onto a sled. Their owner mushed them away.

Sled dogs, highly trained and uncharacteristically silent, threw extreme vigor into their work in a fashion reminiscent of Alaska's famous Iditarod sled race.

The ice held for them. Soon, they crossed the ice bridge to the smaller of the two islands. Toward safety.

• • •

"There they are! Shoot them!" shouted the Russian major. "Kill them!"

"They are in America!" yelled his lieutenant.

No one fired.

The major ripped the rifle from the man and turned. He'd demonstrate leadership. As he turned, he smiled. It was premature.

The rescuer had placed charges—heavy charges—at the Russian end of the bridge. As the officer moved forward to take aim, he stepped on a squeaky-toy. The squeak activated a time-delayed succession of C-4 charges. In addition, the squeak warned.

The charges, too small to kill the soldiers, were large enough to fracture the ice bridge. It creaked and groaned for a few seconds as the men made for Mother Russia. Right behind the dogs.

Once he was safe, the major turned. The whiteout had swept back in. He saw nothing.

• • •

The dogsled arrived at the American island's only village. There, in a prepared safe-house, the intelligence operative was triaged. Reintroduced to life. To warmth. He would not learn until much later that the man who'd risked his own life to bring him and his precious intelligence back to America—to perhaps save millions of lives—was the special one. Codename: Magic Man.

CHAPTER 1

While life as it was had continued on in the outer reaches of American sovereignty, the operative who'd survived the unendurable had received suitable triage, rest, and recuperation, at least according to someone farther up the administrative chain.

Upon arrival at the National Security Agency's ultra-secretive Maryland headquarters, he'd been relieved of the top secret device he'd liberated from the Russian island outpost. Although not deemed anywhere near ready for any future NSA operative duty, his superior declared him well enough for the final phase of his covert operation.

Now began the exploration of that which only he had seen and done. The digital interrogation. The mind phase.

The enclosure was new. Its 30-foot diameter and Arctic White coloration made a quick and lasting visual impression. Its placement in the middle of a very large box of a room with no windows provided no context.

One installer remarked that the multitude of depressions across its entire spherical surface gave it the appearance of a golf ball. The man even suggested painting Titleist, a popular brand, in strategic locations to finish the effect.

While the Golf Ball's promotional documentation indicated exceptional psychological and operational promise, it was experimental just the same. In fact, this was the first time a real operative and a real operation were combined to test the engulfing nature of the experience.

Medical staff stood close by. They didn't expect problems. Their presence was SOP. Standard Operating Procedure.

Disrupting the normal calm in the outer structure, the doors of the dimpled spherical chamber burst open. Men and women, dressed in tight-fit, steel-blue jump suits, rushed inside to the unconscious man at its center.

He lay on a rubberized floor, tethered there by very special shoes.

An Emergency Medical Services specialist released the shoe clasps.

She straightened his legs.

The lead medic clipped leads onto metal nipples affixed beforehand to the downed man's chest. He shouted, "*Clear!*"

All stepped back.

The lead applied a minor charge through the defibrillator. With a wave of his arm and no words spoken, he led his team out.

The subject stiffened to a sitting posture, gasping air between hacking coughs.

A large red LED clock above the door counted time.

In seventeen seconds, his pulse slowed to normal. Remarkable.

A man in the periphery stepped to within ten feet. "A pretty heavy experience, no?"

The subject glared up at him. "That was me. In the virtual reality. That was the environment I experienced. The whiteout. The shooting. The dogs. This … this …"

"It's the new DVD—Déjà Vu Device."

"… this contraption caused me to relive …"

His pulse ramped to a much higher level.

He huffed and puffed, aware that the experiment had penetrated inside his mind.

The man waved forward an assistant with a cool wash cloth, motioning for it to be placed on the subject's forehead.

After a few minutes, it produced a calming effect.

As the other man approached, the subject reclined and summarized his experience. "In one way, I feel like a victim more than the subject of an experiment. In another, I feel like the post-pubescent male awakened from a very special dream ... by his mother. There's the shock of snapping into consciousness ... and then the indecency of it all."

"What about this particular dream—actually a replay of reality?"

The self-described victim stared up into the man's eyes. "It was as if my direct superior had sent me there to be killed. Eliminated."

The standing man's crooked mouth formed a smile. He checked his badge.

Andrew Scott.

"Direct superior? That would be me."

CHAPTER 2

To the far west of the contiguous forty-eight states, a small coastal town called San Ernestino stretched alongside the north-south coastal road known as Highway One. Over the years, the town steadily spread east to a freeway known by Southern Californians as The Five. In fact, all freeways were numbered and almost never referred to by any textual name given them. Some years in the past, people known as Angelinos invented this means of labeling freeways. One frequently heard The Ninety-One or The Two-Ten on the radio or in conversation. The rare exception: Highway One.

Heading south on Highway One this particular night, a muddied black truck, at least twenty-years old, passed through a tiny residential suburb, and then through the business district of San E itself. All legal business took place on this street. Bicycle store, craft store, clothing boutique, mom-and-pop restaurant, and other similar fare—all locally owned—constituted the range of choice for locals and tourists alike.

The truck's driver scoffed. For him, tonight's operation had nothing in common with the word, legal.

Leaving downtown, the highway passed bluffs on the right, some vacant land, a lone house, and more vacant land. Had the driver continued, he would've followed the road as it dropped down to sea level into the small town of Runon Beach. At sea level, he could have rolled down his window and heard the crashing of waves as they cascaded onto the eastern edge of the Pacific Ocean.

Not even a heaven full of stars could light up the summer sky without the moon's help, and no moon glowed that night. The air felt particularly dry, belying the huge ocean less than a mile to the west. Sparse energy-efficient street lamps some 200 yards distant in either direction barely illuminated the single-story cliff-side home that had basked in the glow of a red-orange sunset a mere six hours ago.

But even a full moon and mercury-vapor lighting would have had trouble exposing the man dressed full in black who crept around the home. His black tactical backpack contained tools of his dark trade. Under orders, he didn't know he was about to start a virtual revolution that would shock a nation.

When he'd arrived a short time earlier, he observed lights in the living room. He knew the architecture—he'd seen the floor plan.

The dark man bided his time until the living room lights gave way to bedroom lights. Then, to darkness.

It was time. He exited his Dodge Ram pickup, and headed onto the property.

No one had shared a rhyme or reason for this deed. He never needed that. He was a professional. Just mission and manner. His Special Operations training and experience in far away lands he wished he could forget took care of the rest.

He approached, listening for dogs and utilizing night-vision goggles to check for their signs. He found none.

A white picket fence enclosed a yard of lumpy Korean grass. He sprayed lubricant on the gate's hinges and latch, then entered.

Warily, he crossed the fifty-foot expanse. He paused for a moment.

Pressing his back against the house, he surveilled the highway.

The lights of infrequent passersby shed no illumination on the operative or his vehicle. He felt a compulsion to light up a smoke to calm his hand tremors. A glow-suppressed electronic cigarette and a ballistic nylon bag served the purpose.

He glanced at his fingers, one hand at a time. The tremors were manageable.

His watch's minute-hand clicked straight up. It was time.

Utilizing a military trenching tool, he dug a small hole under the side of the house.

He knew there were alarms inside, and he hoped they were in good operating order. After all, the inhabitants' lives would depend on it. And they were required to survive.

The device he took from his pack was small and dark gray in color. It contained a chemical known to firefighters as accelerant.

He set a timer on the device to detonate at 5:38 A.M. Sunrise.

Before leaving the scene, he bowed his head and said a brief prayer as he always did. He prayed not for success, but for the well-being of his victims.

• • •

The news of the explosion and fire at the Han residence made it into print before the end of the day. The house sustained damage, but could be repaired. Mister and Misses Han, awakened by their alarm system, grabbed a satchel of photographs and escaped to a safe distance.

The fire department, notified quickly by the alarm company, arrived only a few minutes after the klaxon blared.

With their usual pomp and circumstance, the town's two fire trucks and sole paramedic unit flashed down the Coast Highway. They resembled steroidal Christmas trees, generating sufficient noise to wake the honorable dead 3,000 miles away in Arlington, Virginia.

The drivers parked all vehicles in a circle, much like early pioneers expecting an attack by hostile Indians. With regard for their equivalent of military rules of engagement, the firefighters stationed them a safe distance from the house in case of a follow-on explosion. Of course, an explosion in the residence might take out all the firefighters, but the town's equipment would remain intact.

The man responsible had now dressed himself in jeans and a western shirt. The previous black apparel was thin and could be slipped on or removed quickly. He had taken it off and placed it behind the truck's seat. Now, he stood down the highway, watching the firemen do what firemen do so well.

He could see the Hans, standing outside. As elderly as they were, they appeared to still be in good working order. Surely their home had sustained significant damage, but he thought that, this time, they received the message his employer was trying to send.

He hoped so. If he had to come back—not good.

He turned and walked back to his truck. It fired up in an instant. He quickly muted the blaring Country music. He needed silence. He would call in to report his success.

CHAPTER 3

Andrew Scott blew through the air-blade doorway at America's NSA intelligence facility as though someone had pissed on his Fruit Loops.

The downdraft, vertical blade of high-pressure air allowed passage, even if encumbered, but prevented sights, sounds, and environment conditioning from crossing between rooms.

So upset, he had forgotten his Detroit Tigers cap. Having his $400 haircut set askew blackened his temperament further.

"Where's that…"

"In the DVD device. The Golf Ball." His Super-Asian assistant, as he called her, remained expressionless, as usual.

"Why the hell…?"

"You said to test him once again with his Big Diomede memories. Now that he's healthy. You said it was to create a reverse baseline for the first test. The one after he—"

"I know what the crap I said."

The red-faced superior of the man being tested stopped dead.

He stared at the one-and-a-half story ball. It had been the top man's great idea and supplanted actual working staff that Scott considered critical. Trudging 300 yards via underground access to their now location, just to check status, made the Golf Ball his enemy.

Much larger than its eponymous cousin, it was white with dimples. He'd asked its cost and had been told that his security clearance lacked the stratospheric elevation for that data. He'd glowed red with anger. And even if he did possess the clearance, he was further informed, he lacked the Need To Know. He'd stomped out of the room.

Reflecting on such experiences didn't bode well for his heart. So said his cardiologist. He knew exactly what to do. He instituted his personal means of calming. "I don't give a flying—"

Without warning, the Ball changed from paper white to pulsing red, notifying the on-alert emergency rescue team.

As they ran toward the curved door, Scott exercised his authority. "Save the son-of-a-bitch! If he's going to die, I'll be the one to do it!"

Moments later, the Emergency Medical Services ambulance emerged, bearing a man strapped to a gurney. His gray jumpsuit bore two rectangular burn marks at chest level. Barely conscious, he moaned.

The man in charge slowed down enough for a one sentence sitrep. "It'll take him at least six hours to recover, Sir. You might want to—"

"He's had plenty of time." Scott checked his watch. "I'll take him. Time to debrief."

• • •

Less than an hour after Kimbel Stones had been pulled again by paramedics from the Golf Ball re-experience environment dubbed DVD for Déjà-Vu Device, he collected his thoughts in his office.

The nerve twitches caused by defibrillation became less frequent. Experience assured him they would go away. He knew his boss wouldn't, though. He sat back and reflected on his circumstance.

• • •

No matter what one called the building, from the outside it appeared as a big glass cube. The black-hued window-tint reflected the sun's rays, but, more important, closed off the operations inside to prying eyes, airborne or otherwise. The dark exterior unintentionally depicted the nature of the work going on within. For inside, there were small personal-sized offices of floor-to-ceiling glass. Like the building's exterior panes, they did not transmit sounds to the outside. Kinetic isolation was the term.

The National Security Agency had long ago determined that prying ears could be frustrated by merely using lasers to capture interior acoustic waves as they bumped into exterior windows. The latest technology vibrated the outside glass, sending disinformation to enemies.

Phones rang frequently in the Black Cube. Communication was the nature of the business. A personal call came into office C217 that afternoon. 'Personal' took on a different meaning here. All calls were monitored. No exceptions.

The man who picked up the phone on the third distinctive hum did not expect this call. As simple and friendly as it seemed, it would transport him 3,000 miles and change his world, and that of a host of others.

The man's masculine appearance at six-feet even was accentuated by his 185 pound, well-cared-for body. That he was handsome, highly educated, and held a steady job would have made him a likely marital prospect.

So far, no woman had succeeded at reining him in. He guarded his own secrets like he guarded those he had taken an oath to protect. He deemed keeping intimate relationships at bay an operational necessity due to the exceptional seriousness of his job. He held a high security clearance, but today's call would not test his tickets.

Dressed in what passed for business casual in D.C., he wore a charcoal Ralph Lauren shirt with the standard red polo player logo embroidered on the left breast. His shoes were shiny black Nunn-Bush loafers, each with two little tassels instead of a penny pouch.

He did not recognize the nervous voice at first, but then it came to him. Of course, a close family friend, Quentin Han. He had not seen the man nor his loving wife for years. He owed them a great deal. He'd planned on squaring his debt, but time had gotten away from him.

"Do you know who this is?" asked the voice.

Stones smiled briefly. The nature of the Agency was to know who was calling before the call was put through. Voice recognition. Gender recognition. Name. Address. Membership on government hit lists. In milliseconds, a complete summary dossier appeared along with numerous icons on his desktop computer screen. He could move from the summary to particulars with a glance and a blink. The Agency computers contained more information on the caller than the caller's mother. This caller ID set his mind at ease.

"Yes, I know it's you, Quentin. It has been too long since I've heard your voice. How the hell are you?"

Quentin finished with the telephone handshake repartee quickly. A screen graphic analyzed the man's breathing. *Caller upset, needs assistance* popped onto the screen next to a heart-rate monitor.

"You're upset. You're supposed to be retired. This isn't my retired friend talking. What is it?"

"I should hang up. It is my problem. I must deal with it as your father would have."

Quentin never asked for favors. "You're right. This isn't like you. All the more important. Please, tell me."

The man finished with his friend in only three minutes and 27 seconds. The call gave him a great deal to consider. He was sorry to hear that things were not going well for the Hans out in California.

Before he could process what he'd been told and formulate a plan, his phone rang again. The man in the corner office—his boss. He hustled out of his work cell, as he called it, and down the hall. He wondered what was so urgent.

As he walked into the corner office, Andrew stood there with a smile. A smile on Andrew's face was something to be appreciated. Smiles did not come easily to the man.

"Not bad work on the Project Crossword thing. I've closed it out with a Level Five—as good as it gets. The old man, who acts sometimes like a woman, has as much as ordered me to give you some time to bask in your own sunshine. My advice is to take it before she lapses into menopause mayhem again. I still don't know why that word begins with *men*, do you?"

The Ralph Lauren man shook his head. Recognizing the opportunity, he smiled and then he spoke, "One year."

"What?" Andrew Scott was not hard of hearing; it was just a reaction.

"I need a year."

"What?"

"I'm headed out to California. I've got a bill to pay."

"I've never been west of Manassas. And California is fine if you can handle the granola people. You know—nuts, fruits, and flakes." Andrew did not laugh. He recalled his boss's admonition, but did not cede authority easily. "I'm sure it's important to you. So, how about we compromise. At one month?" he asked in his most accommodating fashion.

"Gotta be a year, boss. I've got a big payback due and these folks…" He held up his cell phone, giving it a shake. "…never ask for help. Help me out so I can put this behind me. Then you have me for what ever dark episode comes up next. This is the only thing on my repay agenda. I need your blessing."

The older man tugged the lapels on his commodore-grade blazer. The man before him had demonstrated his ability to achieve results via mental or physical means as demanded by a particular situation. In short, he always succeeded. Subordinates like him weren't anyone's creation. They were the evolution of an inherent talent.

"You're lucky, Stones. We've got a rare lull in your area of expertise, and the old man would simultaneously water board and cattle prod me if she knew I didn't kiss you on both cheeks and give you a bag of Peanut M & M's for your trip. But don't be surprised if you come back in exactly one year or less, and I have a three-year stint arranged for you back on Little Di. I am, of course, referring to the Bering Strait island of Little Diomede. You do recall it, don't you?"

With assistance from the Golf Ball, Stones remembered being within an eye-lash of death like it was yesterday. "I've tried to forget."

Andrew Scott nodded, but wouldn't let it go. He felt the encroachment of his superior on the A. Scott personal fiefdom. "From there you could, with the naked eye, see its sister island, Big Diomede, couldn't you? Not only do a few miles of ice cold sea water separate the two, but big sister belongs to…"

It irritated Stones to no end that his boss made it a habit to extract facts they both knew. "The Russian Federation."

"Yeah, Sarah, you *can* see Russia from Alaska. If you're standing on Little Diomede. And it's not as isolated as it sounds. Hell, in 2006, a couple of guys walked over the ice to Siberia. Getting interested?"

"I'm only alive because of that other operative."

"Ouch. Bailed out by someone not even from our Agency. Don't forget that. Remember that you have been on borrowed time ever since that operation. Now get out of here and head out to that silly West Coast where the only excitement… there isn't any. And don't screw up. Or your next trip to Diomede will be one way. Shoot, you may just get married there and have kids. Of course you'll have to go to the mainland to find a wife, but the Bering Straight School District is right up there. About 150 Inupiat natives for company. And 2.8 square miles to wander around in. They say you can see polar bears float by on the ice flows. Are you getting the drift of this lesson in geography? You are back here in exactly 365 days or your zip code will change to 99762. Clear? The only 900-hundred number you will be able to get will be 907, and they don't talk sex."

"Thanks, Andrew, for the data dump on Diomede. If I have to retire some day from my post on Little Di, it will be worth it."

Director Scott drew a deep breath and exhaled slowly. He checked his watch. "Starting… now!" were his parting remarks.

The Ralph Lauren polo shirt and its inhabitant turned. He left the office. The new Rules of Engagement, thanks to the old man, were go home, pack, and take the first flight out to the West Coast. Assured in his mind that the days—for now—of bullets and mayhem were set aside, he said, as if delivering a tongue-in-cheek warning, "California, here comes Kimbel Stones."

CHAPTER 4

Despite double insulation in the walls and windows, the Russian general could not ignore the howl outside. His adjutant helped him on with the polar bear-fleeced, floor-length coat.

The much younger man attempted to open the door in a dignified manner, but the exterior bluster won out. The heavy steel door slammed open, throwing him over a desk.

He jumped to his feet as if everything was normal, and joined his commandant.

The remainder of the headquarters staff applied every ounce of their collective energy to shut the foul weather outside.

The pair trudged over packed ice and snow the 150 feet to the helipad. Over the crunch of feet and the wind, the general posed a solitary question.

"What's the forecast?" he yelled as he brushed the snow from his eyes.

"I am sorry, Sir. What?"

The general repeated himself.

His aide accentuated an up-and-down head shake. "Compared to where you're going, this is Miami Beach."

"This operation is so important, I'm expected to travel in a helicopter? In these conditions?" He raised his arms, then dropped them, to punctuate his frustration and concern.

The aide, with his personal closeness to the powerful man next to him, knew it was his duty to bear the brunt of all bad news. Changing the general's foul mood would gain him favorable points.

"If it's any consolation, Sir, the fixed-wing aircraft have been grounded."

The general managed an evil look.

"Sorry."

He pressed his superior up the stairway and inside, completing the operation with a crisp salute. The general motioned an airborne medic out of the best seat and slunk into it.

He glared at his adjutant one last time as a ground crew member pulled the door closed.

• • •

As the general's helicopter from the Russian coastal town of Uelen—just 33 miles northwest of his destination—approached, he caught sight of an oversized landing platform. The target's size gave him little solace as his transportation buffeted side-to-side with the brisk winds, finally banging down near one edge.

With his adjutant following, he escaped rather than alighted, and jumped into a militarized 4x4 pickup, which drove him down a ramp into the island's plateau center.

Inside, the base commander—a colonel—greeted him with a crisp salute. His own facial muscles expressed themselves in a quite unpleasant fashion.

The commander led them through steel double-doors, then down a long corridor to an office. "Follow me, but say nothing," he told his aide, who closed the office door behind to the clunk of an electronic bolt.

The general tossed his valise on the other man's desk with a thud.

"It doesn't please me to have to come here, Colonel."

"Sir, welcome to..." His heart pounded within his tunic. He discarded the pleasantries, and spoke quick, and soft. "My senior officers let me down, let us all down. You see, it wasn't my fault."

The much thinner man glanced around the room, then raised his voice. "And my troops languish here 7,500 kilometers—4,600 American miles—from Moscow, and morale is at bottom."

"And because of what happened here with your morale-challenged force far from the reach of our dear president, Vladimir, I have to leave the comfort of my fine offices and apartments, fly to this God-forsaken place in blizzard conditions to see for myself, and return with a report."

"There is good news, General. The weather is turning. In three days, we shall have sun. We expect a low of three degrees centigrade until then. And even better news. I hereby personally apprise you that the American operative was surely killed, and that our state secrets are safe."

"What did the spy take?"

"What was stolen by the American, General Roskov, were our Top Secret plans for Operation Seward. They are heavily encrypted."

"That is good news. Assure me there will be no repeat of this vulnerability."

"I do. Uh, perhaps you would excuse your number two, so we may talk in private." His eyes framed it as a question.

"I selected him myself. His credentials and devotion to Russia are not to be questioned."

"Very well. An American breached our perimeter."

Frustrated, the general raised his voice. "I already know that. This man breached everything and escaped. Surely, you sent forces when the alarm sounded."

That the alarm system had been monitored in Moscow caused the colonel's lip to twitch. "Our force sallied into a wailing blizzard with dogs. Since there are no civilians on the island and no patrols, the men fired at any sound. He couldn't have survived."

"Do you have the body?"

"I'm sorry to say this. Very sorry. No. It was lost to the snow and ice. Rest assured, General. We will find it, and anything he took, when the thaw comes in July."

"I don't think you realize how important our Operation Seward is. I was dispatched here by Russia's top military officer."

The commander realized his subservient approach wasn't winning over the general. He moved to a position of strength. "With due respect, please don't lecture me, Sir. I have thirty-three years of service."

"In addition, Colonel, I was sent with the blessings of the highest official in our *Federalnaya Sluzhba Bezopasnosti*."

The other man's eyes went wide at mention of the FSB. "But that is our internal counter-espionage entity." The colonel felt perspiration in the wrong places. "We will find a means of locating the man. I will report back immediately."

"I don't think so."

"Surely—"

"Our external espionage entity has discovered that the man who came here alone, and treated himself to our uppermost state secret, is alive and well. Most likely on a sunny Southern California beach, as we speak."

"*Sluzhba Vneshney Razvedky*? The SVR? That's impossible. He must be dead." The colonel's lip twitch exceeded his control.

The general motioned to his number two. "By the way, he's extra loyal. He's my cousin."

The commander's next words were poorly chosen. "With due respect, Sir, nepotism will kill us all."

"No, Colonel. Just you."

The adjutant, a major, moved quickly to the colonel, and jerked his arm up.

The colonel's face turned pale. His jaw dropped.

The younger man forced a Makarov pistol into his hand, and affected the trigger pull.

The unsilenced report brought the guards.

Seeing their dead commander with a smoking gun in his hand and their general safe, they quickly shouldered their AK-47's and dragged the corpse from the room.

The door banged shut behind them.

"Nicely done, cousin." The general stood and moved to his relative.

He retrieved two items from his pants pockets and replaced the major's epaulets. "Field promotion. Full Colonel. You're in charge."

The proud general provided his dumbfounded relative the requisite Russian Army *you're safe for now* hug. Smiling, he then stepped through the only other door in the office.

Having taken barely fifteen minutes to relieve himself, the general reversed his arrival sequence, noticing in the distance the firing squad execution of the force that had allowed the American operative to escape. He proffered a broad smile. Cousin was nothing if not efficient.

CHAPTER 5

Kimbel R. Stones had reserved the next flight to Los Angeles out of Dulles International Airport, west of Washington, D.C. He'd worked at a proprietary in Herndon—a stones throw from Dulles—and knew his way around that section of Virginia. An NSA colleague had described their outside-the-grid entities, proprietaries, as unholy-owned subsidiaries. It had been an attempt at humor, but accurate nonetheless.

As he blew by the little town in one of the ubiquitous hardened black SUV's, he observed several huge tanks full of JP5 jet fuel used for refueling the commercial birds. Such tank farms seemed available targets for evil-doers. Those in charge didn't seem to mind.

Dispatched frequently, the passenger jets at Dulles looked like a shiny silver flock executing a Chinese fire drill.

Stones knew his way around the airport. He found a spot, knowing its classified GPS beacon would attract the appropriate pick up crew from the office.

After blowing through the pre-TSA meet and greet, he found himself race walking toward the gate. He slowed. Even his impressive credentials couldn't get the aircraft to board any sooner.

But all was not bad. His collection of frequent flyer points, created at will by NSA operatives, provided him a first-class upgrade so he did not have to eat his knees throughout the five hour flight westward.

Finally aboard, he stepped down his constitutional single-malt Scotch a notch to a blended whisky Johnny Walker Red on the rocks. To him it tasted more like a Johnny Smith or Johnny Jones plus a dash of dish water, but it did the job. A couple of those and the flight attendants still did not look good. It would've taken more.

It didn't matter. His mission was personal. This one mattered to him every bit as much as his National Defense work.

"Sir?" The flight attendant waited a beat to deploy her attitude. "Sir? Seat belts are required, even in First Class."

He attempted to wrest the belts from underneath, noticing that the attendant held one hand behind her back as if nurturing a taser.

"There." He completed the cincture. "Would you consider joining me for dinner?" Under his breath, he cursed the alcohol. He was single, but not that single.

She leaned down. "Forgive me, sir. We're not allowed to use profanity with our passengers. Give me a moment to think of something else freezing over."

He watched her move to the row behind and caught a glimpse of the rectangular black item she held behind her back. Still, he supposed that being tased would be preferable to being shot.

Stones reached to his side and felt the bandage underneath his shirt. A quick glance at his hand assured him that his Diomede wound had not re-opened. He smiled, clamped the headrest wings next to his head, and fell asleep.

• • •

John Wayne International Airport is not in Los Angeles County, but most people don't know that. Those not from Southern California tend to think of everything south of San Francisco as Los Angeles. Not so. The John Wayne, as locals called it, is actually in Orange County, the county famous for housewives with more money than sense and looks, and a complete absence of orange trees.

Kimbel rented appropriate wheels—a BMW 640i xDrive convertible—for the 72-degrees Fahrenheit, partly cloudy ambience. It was the obvious reason ragtops were so popular in this part of the state.

The trip south on The Five freeway terminated with the moderate-sized spa town of Carlsbad. Kimbel took the freeway off ramp onto Cannon Road and headed west. The BMW's clock, accurate or not, signaled 5:30 in the afternoon as he turned south again onto the famous coast road—Highway One.

As the sun descended toward the horizon, it produced a beautiful reddish hue that lit the prevailing cloud cover to fine art quality. The Pacific Ocean appeared a dark blue and the smell of the sea air wafted into the convertible.

Kimbel Stones enabled a device he carried in his shirt pocket. In the next few seconds, a pleasant voice provided operational intel.

"Continuing on to Ventria. A smallish coastal town known for surfing and surfers. Recommend you not stop for food. The local fare is limited to light drugs and chips."

The magic of his employer, the NSA, was that in a few milliseconds, satellites and road cameras picked up his license, applied facial recognition to his countenance, and provided dialog content far exceeding that of standard GPS. Since some people might take offense, the Agency didn't publicize the true extent of its capabilities.

"ETA?"

"Three-point-four-seven-nine minutes," the voice replied. "Would you prefer a countdown?"

"Negative on the countdown." Stones felt certain such dialog would attract attention. "Closing GPS."

"Oh," came a pout. "Another time?"

At this hour, the roadsides were still replete with men and women of all ages riding bicycles—surfboard under an arm—heading *toward* the beach, not *away*. Like Carlsbad inland, coastal Ventria rose just above sea level. It vied with Hawaii for numbers of palm trees. South of town, Stones started to climb uphill toward San Ernestino, where his long-time friends, the Hans, resided.

San E, as locals called it, occupied the top of a sea bluff that rose some sixty-seven feet above the ocean at high tide. It made getting down to the beach quite dangerous, but patient, athletic beachgoers descended the narrow and steep path to a relatively vacant beach. Alternatively, they could continue on the coast road further south to Runon Beach, which returned them to sea level. There, they would park. They walked along the ocean edge two miles to the pristine white sand beaches below the San E bluff.

It was on the bluff, just before the dropdown to Runon, that the Hans lived. They had three level acres and a to-die-for view of the Pacific. If God had not put Hawaii so far away, they could have seen it from their back yard. They had purchased their home just before the steep price inclines that began in 2003. The first evidence of San E that Kimbel spotted was the usual sign, which said, "You Are Now Entering San Ernestino. Population: 11,231."

The town resembled numerous coastal California towns. The houses were of eclectic design on large lots. East toward The Five, one could see a few condominium parks and housing tracts. On the sunup side of the ridgeline, most lacked an ocean view. The small shops in the business district were juxtaposed and typical of 1950's and 1960's architecture. The sensation, like stepping back into a more quiet and calming time.

Kimbel's focus kept him centered on the present. He just could not wait to see Quentin and Bettie again. It had been too many years.

A mile beyond the business district, Kimbel pulled right into the Hans driveway. What he saw caused him to stop. The side of the house was black and broken. Sheets of plywood covered the breach. Clearly, a blast and fire. Slowly, he drove close enough to back his vehicle onto the front yard.

He had called the Hans from John Wayne Airport and they had set out the welcome mat. He'd hardly stopped before the shorter, older man was tugging at the door handle.

After hugs and pleasantries, the Hans situated Kimbel and his luggage into their second bedroom. They tried to give him their master bedroom, but Kimbel firmly declined.

After dinner, the three talked at length. Then, Kimbel stole thankfully to bed. A long day's journey and the three-hour time difference had taken the wind out of his sails. And there would always be tomorrows.

• • •

Kimbel spent the next two weeks repairing and painting outside, cleaning out the garage, and all the other items left undone since the onset of Bettie's illness.

He expressed his interest in the area, and Quentin Han urged him to stop by the local newspaper and do a little research. Quentin figured his status as a paid up subscriber should get Kimbel first class treatment. Then, Quentin winked.

It sounded good. Kimbel was deluged with data and information at work, knew the difference between the two, and knew his way around the stuff. He thanked his parents' old friend, stating he would drive into town the very next day.

CHAPTER 6

Silas Treadwell held the title Executive Editor. It meant he ran the local newspaper in the small Southern California town called San Ernestino. There were two big regionals in Los Angeles and San Diego, but nothing of note in the two small neighboring coastal towns that bookended San E.

Since the regionals were in large cities and a number of miles distant, they didn't connect with small town people. And since the editor's previous experience was with local papers that really didn't connect with the people, he didn't see a problem. He succeeded by securing all local advertising, local human interest stories, the classifieds, and then filled the rest of the space with wire stories.

He pulled into the parking lot behind the *Observer* on a day like most any other. 72 degrees, partly cloudy, and a gentle sea breeze blowing in from the west. Ho hum. He felt a sense of personal pride at being a stalwart version of the vaunted Fourth Estate. All activities of the daily paper took place in a single-story industrial building, the exception being that the reporters went out in the field for their stories. They returned with particulars relating to the latest lost pet or stolen hubcap crisis. His little town.

Entering from the rear, one of his favorite things to do, he walked through the production room where stories and advertising underwent the conversion into a tabloid-like paper product. Activity started there at 6:30 every morning, concluding at 4:30 when the paper had been put to bed. He felt it important to honor his prestigious position by showing up a few minutes earlier than everyone else. Shortly thereafter, employees pulled into the parking lot, and filed inside.

Through the door ahead was the Ballroom, otherwise known as the City Desk. To the immediate left was the desk for the copy boy and another desk for a person who covered the local social scene. Directly before him sat a triangle of three desks. Two desks for the reporters, the third for the City Editor.

To his right was a small private office, within which resided the sole proofreader. The ratification of punctuation, grammar, syntax, continuity, and elevation of stories to the paper's high standards still made the task seem less complicated than necessary. On the other hand, it might have been the most necessary job in the building. It determined what the customers saw.

In size, the Ballroom was double that of a school classroom and exceptionally well lighted. Rows of industrial strength fluorescent lights overhead assured that no shadows could conceal any evidence of sloth.

When Silas Treadwell was not serving the God-like purpose that is the City Editor, he resided in the only other private office, located in the far left corner of the building, when viewed from the back. If one entered the front door, his office as Managing Editor would be to their right. The thick front door was made of steel and the building had no windows. The architect, which is like calling a fry cook a chef, had either worried that employees would be tempted to gaze out the windows, or that their contribution to the town's look and feel needed to be one of a late 1950's bomb shelters.

On this day, Silas entertained the possibility of hiring an additional reporter. Hiring and firing was his most formal duty. On this day, he'd dressed to that purpose. He sported a clean and lightly starched white dress shirt buttoned at the collar. With that, his favorite and only tie—burgundy and gold diagonal stripes. The slacks were of silver color and had been pressed only a week before. To top it all off, on his feet were his only pair of shoes: sandals by Nunn Busch. Now sandals by themselves were not exactly dressy, not even in a beach town. He'd added a pair of black dress socks to finish off the look.

Silas had barely sat down when a bell clanged in the front of the office. The demi-klaxon bell ingress and egress to and from the building was a holdover from the early days, which fit the editor's style.

In an attempt to ignore it, he began to edit some exceptionally boring copy. Since editing was his City Editor job, he felt compelled to loosen his tie and unbutton his collar. He looked up after several minutes, as if expecting a patter of feet to greet whoever had entered the hallowed, albeit cozy, asylum. There was none. He pushed back his long out-of-style editor's chair, nearly tripping over the seat cushion that never stayed in place. He'd have to fix that someday.

He opened the oak door that normally protected the sanctity of the Owner/Managing Editor. He turned to see a handsome man about six feet tall, dressed comfortably, but business-like, looking around for someone who cared. When no one else cared, that meant Silas. As luck would have it, the entire front office staff, all four of them, had decided to take a collective union-like break that left the guest with no-one with whom to interact. The chain of command simplified when there was only one person left.

"Nice to meet you. Sorry, our greeter is on break. You can't go around treating people like those damned phone-tree recordings do. The ones where they say how important you are to them, then put you on hold for forty minutes." He extended his hand. "I'm Silas Treadwell, the editor here. And you…"

"Kimbel Stones."

Silas apologized again and wondered, *What do they do to unimportant people?*

Out of either kindness or self-defense, Stones interrupted with, "I feel the same way—I'm here for the job."

"Job? What job? We're just a small paper and—oh, the political reporting," Silas said as he nimbly retrieved the relevant recalcitrant brain cells. "Yeah, step into my office. I've got my own coffee pot. Please, just help yourself."

Stones followed him into the office. Silas grabbed his coffee mug. He noticed the new prospect glance at the mug and confessed, "I didn't really get any closer to NASA than the tube, but the mug was a gift from someone special." As he turned, the two collided at the coffee station.

Both said, "I'm sorry," and laughed, breaking the usual initial tension.

The editor was not formal in procedure. As they stood over the coffeemaker, he led with, "You know much about politics?"

"I spent quite a bit of time in Washington, D.C. The work was classified, but I wrote up some of the projects I worked on."

"Those long, long government documents? We are, of necessity, terse here. Less is more, I always say."

Kimbel checked out the large, red letters on the far wall: LIM. It brought a smile. "I provided the equivalent of an executive summary for each of the documents. Believe me, they were terse and to the point. I am confident I would be able to write copy for the local market. Because I've spent some serious time on the Southern California coast, I wouldn't need to get the feel for it. I'm excellent at observation and write pretty well, I've been told."

"Sure you can," Silas countered. "Turn around."

Stones turned his back.

"Alright, describe me."

"Fat . . . ugly . . ."

"Hmmm. A sense of humor, have we? Come on. We're on the clock here, Mr. Stones."

"Old enough for Vietnam; young enough to have only read about Korea. Five foot ten. Sexy hairline. Clean, but used white shirt. You wear a tie that someone gave you—he or she was not your friend. Collar open at the top: a sign that you were performing your City Editor role when I arrived. Gray slacks that have more creases running horizontally than vertically, although there are more than two of the latter. Brown sandals over socks that match the job, but not the wardrobe."

Stones removed the brief smile as he turned back to face the editor.

Silas smiled. "So what's not to like?"

"About you?" Stones arched his eyebrow.

"No. About you?"

Stones hoped to get the job without using his NSA boss as a reference. He let the question slide. "I can do the job. I'm available. I accept reasonable compensation."

"You're certainly articulate enough for a local rag. You have a sense of humor uncolored by the fact that you're here for a job. I don't really need another fair-complected Caucasian male for meeting my PC-compliance requirements. I *have* two women who remind me of Christine McVie and Stevie Nicks of Fleetwood Mac, a Vietnamese immigrant who's the most polite person I have ever known, and a Hispanic male that looks like a bowling ball on steroids. I have nothing to lose."

Stones said nothing.

"We're too small a business for foreplay. You're hired," came the bottom line from the editor's tired throat. "It's Monday. Come back tomorrow, and we'll get you started. By the way, you are covering the Mayor's council meeting tomorrow afternoon. Dress for the occasion. We go to press on Wednesday, so we'll need the copy to proofing by seven. That's seven in the morning. Any questions?"

"Payday?" Stones asked.

"Second Friday. First time, this week. Bring in all the particulars tomorrow when you come in."

The two men shook hands. Stones thanked him, turned, and walked out the door.

Silas Treadwell had a habit of talking, even with no listener present. In his office, he'd talk to a replica Oscar statuette given to him by a former actress.

He turned to the statuette. "I liked him right away, Oscar. Call it instinct. But that's how we newspaper guys survive. Equal parts skill, saavy, and instinct. He was the right guy. In fact, I sensed he was more than the right guy."

Just how *much* more would play out over the next few months and leave the weathered newsman, who possessed copious amounts of life experience and thought he had seen it all, just shaking his head.

CHAPTER 7

Treadwell usually rose at five-thirty and arrived at work just over an hour later. Since he was the one with the key, he opened up every day but Sunday, when the newspaper was closed. He didn't have anything against working on Sunday—hell, God worked on Sunday—he just couldn't go up against the big papers' fat Sunday editions with all of those glorious advertising inserts. So, 'take a day off' became his motto of convenience.

This particular Tuesday was not like the others. Kimbel Stones waited inside the front door. He had an envelope in his hand and wore a toned-down light gray suit. He might just have well been wearing a bright yellow zoot suit with a black and purple striped tie. Suits got noticed at local town hall meetings and it appeared as if Kimbel wanted the mayor, her staff, and concubines to take notice the first time. If Treadwell had a crystal ball, he would have paid him for the day and told him to go forth and have a nice life. Elsewhere.

"How the hell…" Treadwell glanced at the man, and then at the door. "I am getting old. Sometimes I guess I forget to lock up. But it's a low-crime town, so no foul."

He gently grasped Stones by the arm. "Come with me. After a little paper work, you're one of us."

Stones had been focused on his first visit. He started to feel a warmth about the place.

"Yes, it's wallpaper, Mr. Stones. I plan on having it cleaned some day."

"If I may, I think the creamy beige color and basket weave texture gives the room a comfortable feel."

"Yeah, well, when my father and I put it up thirty years ago, it was blue."

"Blue."

"And if you look up high, you'll see further evidence we don't clean enough around here."

Stones observed strands of spider web in several places.

"Those belong to Charlotte."

Without warning, a ringing bell klaxoned beyond the room.

"Fire?"

"No. Out of paper in the press room. This building was abandoned by a previous newspaper. They'd gone union. My father and I acquired it and made it work."

"I take it I won't be joining a union."

"You won't be mentioning one, either. You could've gotten by with the Union of Soviet Socialist Republics, but I hear they're not around any more."

Stones nodded affirmation. He also considered that the USSR replacement, the new Russia, might have reason to seek him out.

A gong-like sound tolled seven times.

"San E was an old stage stop. Then the coastal train. The clock tower's at the station." Stones paused for a moment. "I'm guessing that you have some strong ties to the town."

"I like that. I didn't make a sound or move an eyelash. You pick up emotion just like that."

"I notice things. Especially little things," Stones said. "That's why I can do well for you."

"My parents arrived here on one of those trains." He stepped to the side. "See this hat tree. The double-billed hunter's cap—ala Sherlock Holmes—belongs to my Ace Reporter of the Month. He gets to wear it, if he chooses."

"There are no women reporters?"

"Good catch. Not yet. I've tried to get Luisa to step in, but she loves her job." Treadwell continued the march to his office. "You ever been in combat, Kimbel?"

Stones recalled the recent skirmish with the Russian forces on Big Diomede. He wondered if that counted. Simple answer. "No. No combat."

"Military?"

Yes, the editor could be succinct. He took another look at the man's balding head, with its askew silver-brown hair, about two inches in length. Itself, succinct.

"No, Sir."

Inside Treadwell's office, the two sat down and recorded all of his payroll trivia. Treadwell noticed his suburban address, which was anything that wasn't zoned commercial. No spouse. No children. Contacts were a Mr. and Mrs. Quentin Han. No matter—Treadwell could delve into particulars later.

"You said yesterday you worked on classified documents..." He left room for his new hire to elaborate.

"They classify them as Confidential, Secret, and Top Secret. After a number of years, they de-classify them to Unclassified." He left out the many details inherent in the secrecy of documents—like Need To Know—and the classifications above Top Secret that were, themselves, classified.

The older man rubbed his chin. "So, if none of them are Unclassified, you can't show them to me so I can check your work. That about right?"

"Their rules, not mine."

"Let's see. No references or work product. Perfect. I'm bringing you in on a wing and a prayer, as my father would've said. You know that, don't you?"

He showed Stones to a used, gray steel government-style desk. "This is your office. Since I believe in team work, I'll show you around. We have 600 square feet of office space," he said, pointing out the desks of Stones' new colleagues. "As you can see, the occupants, unlike legitimate news hounds, have a respect for promptness that makes Hawaiians look like New Yorkers in comparison."

"I've not been to Hawaii, Mr. Treadwell."

With a motion of his hand, Managing Editor Treadwell bade Kimbel Stones follow him.

"This is where our reporter dwells, Kimbel. His name is Tram Nguyen. Formerly the only reporter, he is now the *other* reporter. We don't have a lot of news." Treadwell shrugged for emphasis. "Tram got off the boat seven years ago. His language skills still could use some work and I, in my less-than-humble way, decided that his interpretation of political inuendo—the things a politicians say when not just lying outright—require far too much post-processing to be worthwhile." The two moved on.

"And this, this is the office of Miss Thomson, Susanna Thomson. She hates Susanna so just call her Susie Cream Cheese." He smiled to himself.

Kimbel nodded as if he had made a mental note, but the editor's expression told Stones to avoid any and all references to cream cheese in his dealings with Susanna.

"I was kidding. She's a terrific advertising girl, but keeps a sharp knife at her desk. I'm sure she would use it on anyone who doesn't call her Miss Thomson or Susanna. She sells our ad space. She also sets up the proofs for our clients to authorize and makes them 'camera-ready' for print production out back."

Treadwell noted that Kimbel was smart. He took in a lot more than he disclosed. Not much hand-holding required here. Treadwell *really* liked him.

"The press guy is in the other room. *El se llama Emilio Lopez*, but you can call him Milo. You can introduce yourself to him some other time."

Treadwell was about to take Stones to the proofreading room when its owner walked in the front door. He leaned to whisper. "Boy, if she doesn't have a way. Maybe five-foot-six. A body that could have played any sport and that moves this way and that when she walks. And as unassuming as you please. If there's an *it* to be had by a woman, she has *it*."

The men stood aside as she walked by. She passed with no more than a nonchalant, but sexually charged "Hello."

Treadwell whispered in Stones' direction, "Remember that old joke: *God gave man a brain and a penis, but only enough blood to work one at a time*? Well that," he opined, as if inspired by Yoda himself, "was Santos. You can call her Luisa. She is sexually off limits, primarily because I saw her first. She's a distraction... and you'd never know she knows."

Kimbel helped Treadwell out of his sexual stupor. "I met a French girl once in Cannes, Mr. Treadwell. I came to learn what the French mean by *je ne sais quoi*. Better than average, more subtle than a centerfold, but most desirable of all."

"A true romantic like myself," Treadwell couldn't help responding. "Luisa's the kind you want to remember last when you die. Come with me."

Kimbel followed his new boss into Luisa's office—the four-by-eight windowless place she called her 'cozy'—and introduced them. He couldn't help remembering from his high school French that, if a man says he wants to *introduce* himself to a woman, he is saying he wants to put himself inside. It pays to do the homework, but he felt that getting slapped by a sexy French lady could be the start of a great 24-hour relationship.

Finished with the orientation tour, Treadwell led the new-hire to his desk and took himself back to his own office. He was behind already—a stack of papers waiting for his perusal and decision-making prowess. He would grab Kimbel again after lunch to prep him for the Town Hall. Once he got a load of the San Ernestino elite, his new hire might just pack up and opt for beach bum over dealing with that bunch.

CHAPTER 8

The intercom on Andrew Scott's office wall rarely spoke. Only one person used the antiquated device. That man happened to be his boss.

"Andy, please stop by at your earliest convenience." Click.

That meant now. He reached his boss' office on the top floor of the NSA Black Cube in three minutes flat. Two knocks. After a loud click, the door pushed open of its own accord. He walked the fifteen feet to an ornate desk and matching chair—from Buckingham Palace during the reign of Elizabeth II—and took a seat.

"Andy, remember the intel Stones filched from the Russian base on Big Diomede?"

Scott gave a nervous twitch, certain that what would follow wouldn't be good. "I do."

"We've achieved a breakthrough on the multiple encryption algorithms used on the data. We have some clear text. Uh, decrypted text."

Scott knew better than call his boss on the obvious: that everyone in the business knew precisely what clear text was.

"Nice. Having them steal our own purpose-built cryptographic algorithms—not wanting to invent their own—works in our favor."

"As a result, I have need for Stones. A very special project. It exceeds Top Secret."

"Uh ..." That got Andrew Scott's attention. Seldom did the NSA engage in operations classified so far above TS that the classifications themselves were classified.

"How soon can you have him in my office?"

"Uh ..."

"Is there a problem?"

"Sir, he's on leave."

"What? This is about America, son. Leave cancelled."

"It's a sabbatical, sir."

"Then cancel that, too." Stanley Coin was not used to pushback.

"A year."

"What?"

"Best friends of his parents—under attack."

"Attack? What attack?"

"It's a civilian matter out on the West Coast. I know him. Pushed, he'll resign."

"Christ on toast." Stanley thought, drawing on his nearly 50 years with the Agency. He'd never been stymied. "Okay. Plan B. I'll read *you* in, establish the mission. Then, it's up to you to execute. Top priority. Are we clear?"

"Yes, sir."

"Here goes. The Russian plan is to take ownership of all Diomede islands. Just like the Crimea. Vladimir wants to be able to see Alaska from his front porch. Of course, we don't give a shit about the islands, but our old pal Vlad believes that the current American president is a coward and has no will to stop him. We have to be careful. He can claim that the Indians and Inuits migrated from Central Asia thousands of years ago and are, therefore, Native Russians."

"So he'd be saying there are no Native Americans."

Stanley nodded affirmation. "Andrew, our mission is to avert a crisis. You tell me here and now you're good to go on the highest clearance allowed by God, and I'll get it for you. Oh, did I bother to say that I'm having my golden anniversary celebration in the near future. You mess this up, and I'll personally shred your balls on a cheese grater. Understand?"

"I'm as American as it gets. We're good on the clearance."

"I don't give a damn about the clearance. What we're good on is the op. With Stones. Period."

CHAPTER 9

Even with the mitigating effect of the Baltic Sea, the autumn temperatures had dropped to unseasonal levels. The first snow, now reduced to wind-swept flurries, glowed in the morning sun.

A cream-colored tanning clamshell burst open.

Out popped a well-tuned, well-tanned, 5'7" 176 pound frame.

"There. Like a golden butterfly—the Monarch—exiting his chrysalis."

Absent a response from the only other person in the room, he stepped outside through lattice windowed double doors.

The tall, slim man with a full beard tried to stay as close as possible to the man on the balcony, yet near to the fireplace and its projected warmth.

"Please come in. Today is an exceptionally important day for you. You mustn't take cold. Your country needs you," he beseeched.

"I am strong, Raspi," blew in from the balcony of the presidential suite.

"We are 633.73 kilometers from the capitol. We must get this done, and return."

"I am aware that any distance from Moscow is a danger to me. Those who would have me dead and buried scheme on an hourly basis."

Raspi began a response, but was cut short.

"How far are we in the English system?"

The presidential advisor, his eyelids blinking as always when he calculated, said, "393.78 miles."

"Now use your mathematical genius to tell me the following: how far from Korsakov?"

The advisor knew what, or who, was in Korsakov in the far east of Russia. He didn't want to go there, but had no choice.

"The city of Korsakov is 6,695.19 kilometers from here."

"In the English."

Again, the eyelids batted. For three seconds.

"4,160.21 miles."

The president turned and stepped inside, closing the windowed shutters as he did.

"You might want to put the shirt back on, Vladimir."

"Yes. It's cold here in St. Petersburg."

"You should stop thinking of her."

"Perhaps she thinks of me."

"Your relationship was some time ago. I'm sure she's moved on."

The younger, shorter man smiled. "She wouldn't forget."

First Advisor Raspi avoided expressing his observations. The president of the Russian Federation had evolved more toward the Michelin Man than the latest American action hero. "The non-Muscovite leaders here are settled in the pews. They await your address. Please be faithful to the teleprompter message as prepared by our psy-ops experts."

"Why do they lean toward this, this Czarina? I've stood Russia tall again. My enduring mantra: *Snova Cdelayut Rossiyu*, Make Russia Great Again, has united our country."

"There is magic in monarchy, Vladimir. Ordained by the gods and all."

"I feel that ordained by me should suffice."

"Well, remember that we are in a religious place, here. Be respectful as you read from the new technology, stained-glass prompter windows as if inspired."

"The resurgence of faith is to blame. There must be only one authority—me."

"Times have changed since the Soviets."

"What if these people reject me? Raspi? What then?"

"Be sure they don't. Stick to the script."

He nodded. With his personal guard under exacting instructions. If the crowd transformed into a mob, he'd duck out the back. His men would once again transform this edifice, hallowed or otherwise, into the Church Of Our Savior On Spilled Blood.

• • •

In an isolated facility in eastern Siberia with Codename: *Uvyortka*—'Dodge' after the American wild-west town—a mid-twenties scientist named Valentina Kummonova jumped up from her seat in a laboratory. "*Da! Ya Znayu!*"

Her boss, in a typical expression of anxiety, lifted his hands—palms and fingertips faced to himself—then pushed them with vigor at her, punctuating his admonition.

"*Angliyskiy, Valya!* English! The service types here do not speak it!"

"Yes! Yes! English! Director, I have discovered the link!"

"No. No. No. You are new. We have pursued this for years, frustrated at every turn."

She held up a triangular-shaped Erlenmeyer flask, swishing its liquid contents. "A mapping of DNA to facial features. To the millimeter."

"Give me that!" The lab leader started toward her.

She suspended the vessel high above the granite floor.

He stopped. Then, backed away.

"A promotion, Sergei? Now?"

"My God. Yes! Yes! Quick." He turned to his second-in-command. "Misha! Get the sample. From the American spy. From Diomede."

Within three minutes, the man returned with a stoppered test tube in hand.

Valya swished the sample, disbursing it evenly throughout her magic liquid. She added a probe attached to a special laptop with an even more special app. Origin unknown.

The three scientists huddled under a black shroud to view the monitor. Their collective heart beats displaced any outside sounds.

A facial structure appeared.

There!

They stood for an extended period, each attempting not to gasp in the others' presence.

"Do it!" Sergei ordered. "Do it now!"

Valya engaged the Identify button on the touch-sensitive screen.

Forty-five excruciating seconds later, an identifying block of data, and a facial image linked to the Diomede DNA sample, filled the screen.

"*Svyashchenniy govno*!"

"*Angliyskiy, Valya!*" Sergei demanded.

"Holy shit!"

"Yes. Holy shit. We now have both ID and features of the Diomede intruder," said the leader. "Alright. Secure link to GRU. Now!"

"The hacking directorate?"

"Now!"

"We need all government and private surveillance in the United States."

"They'll want our ..." Misha glanced back at the screen. "... Kimbel Stones facial map."

"So they can control the search ..."

"... and claim credit."

"Solitary link. Authority: Codename: Marlboro Man. That's right," he said to their wide-eyed stares. "Vladimir. The president himself. No strings."

"What will you do with all that credit if you locate this Stones?"

"We will not merely locate. We will localize and track with software commandeered from our anti-submarine warfare science. What shall I do? Get the hell out of Dodge."

"This may take a great deal of time," Valya advised.

"I see. I'm taking you two with me—"

"Hey!" Valya interrupted. "Got the link. Going live on the face-finder."

• • •

Two hours later, Sergei lapsed back into his normal frustrated mood. "This is hopeless."

Valya gave her head a heavy shake sideways. "Adding my own plug-in. Grabs all phone cameras."

Forty-five minutes later, Valya cried, "Hit! Him! 98% confidence factor! Nearest cell tower ... got it!" She turned to the director she'd just startled awake. She smiled. "Call Vlad!"

• • •

Sergei stepped out of the room for the encrypted, private conversation of his life. When he returned, he held his phone in one hand and a silenced Makarov pistol behind his back in the other. "I have him. I forgot to tell you. I don't share."

He fired one bullet into Misha's head. He knelt to assure the death of his number two.

"Vlad and I had a thing in college," Valya offered from behind him, apparently unfazed by the murder.

Sergei stiffened. He heard her pull something from a drawer. A glance over his shoulder nearly stopped his heart.

"He did some *Mokriye Dela*. Wet Work." She continued, "A Bulgarian. Carved 'V & V' into the man's chest. Vladimir and Valentina. A romantic."

Sergei tensed. He still had a chance.

She was faster. Her shot did stop his heart.

In an hour, she was outbound. Five thousand miles from home. To a place in California.

CHAPTER 10

General Roskov was definitely the man whom Moscow would deem responsible for the Big Diomede intelligence disaster. The Russian president refused to use the man's name, lest its mention caused his head to explode. Raspi, who'd been with Vladimir for quite some years, found it prescient to listen as well to the mood as he did to the words.

"Has anyone seen the general? Since?"

"It's easy to hide in eastern Siberia, Mr. President."

"I'd order Spetsnaz from Moscow branch, but I don't hate any of them enough to send them to our easternmost outpost."

The Russian president's closest advisor, and descendant of the illustrious Rasputin, nodded agreement. "It would simply be revenge. The cat, as Americans say, is out of bag."

It annoyed the top man in Russia that his First Advisor, fluent in English, still left out the definite and indefinite articles, as they did not exist in his birth language. "First, I happen to enjoy revenge. I even schedule it periodically just as a feel good. Second, the CIA and NSA couldn't have decrypted our superior algorithms yet. From what the SVR tells me, it could take them ten years."

"Regretfully, the SVR head needs to say that."

"Certainly…"

The First Advisor cut him off with a twist of his head.

"When, Raspi, am I due for revenge next?" The president waved him off. "Rhetorical."

"He's in the ante-room now, waiting to brief you."

The door opened to allow a broadly-built, tall man to enter. Just from appearances, he seemed descended from another Yuri. His large, bespectacled namesake had been the longest running head of the KGB—from 1967 until 1982. Also orphaned at age 13, this new incarnation of Yuri Andropov caused the president to feel in the company of ghosts. A few seconds without dialog sent the message. The SVR head was on the chopping block. Every word counted.

"Your report, Yuri."

"Our research team has returned from our Diomede site. Due to protocols, we had to include FSB members since the island is domestic. They searched for fingerprints, body fluids, and were kept out of the way."

"Any trace in the facility of who did this?"

The SVR head's left eye twitched. "None. We searched the island. Covered with snow and in sub-zero temperature… we found nothing."

"Then there was nothing left to find. Our strategy for code name Blood Red Ice Cube can be exposed. We must move up our timetable."

Raspi experienced an epiphany. "What if we could locate the one who breached our security and stole the intelligence, Mr. President?"

"What, one of the myriad CIA spies traipsing the planet?"

The SVR head saw himself at the moment as a man who stands on a gallows platform, the rope clawing at his neck, the hangman just grasping the lever.

"There was something. In their thoroughness, the FSB examined the guard dogs—those who had chased the American."

"They probably had sex with the dogs. So what?"

"A speck. Just one."

"A speck? What do I care about a speck when my entire legacy is at stake?" He clasped a letter opener once owned by Czar Nicholas.

Raspi grabbed the SVR head by the arm, yanking him toward the door.

"Blood."

The president stopped cold.

The spymaster tore away from the advisor, pulled a sealed envelope from his jacket, and handed it over.

The president exhaled before ripping it open. With Raspi peering over his shoulder, Vladimir devoured the two words.

"Kimbel Stones."

CHAPTER 11

The White House Chief-Of-Staff, or COS, carried the black folder in both hands. It wasn't that it was heavy, it was the sensitive material therein. He placed it on the president's desk with a delicacy normally reserved for lace panties.

"Here it is. TOP SECRET – POTUS Eyes Only."

"I guess they don't make a TOP SECRET – GOD clearance, so I suppose this is the highest."

"Very funny, Sir. It's the one about Alaska."

"I'm preparing to seek re-election in a year, and you tell me, Cleveland, that Russia wants our 49th state. How absurd."

"How's that, Sir?"

"Every time I come in here, someone's shoving their dick up my butt. I feel like I've got the Oval Orifice."

"Sir?"

"I'm sorry. Cleve. How's that?"

The COS nodded, then continued. "The intel is indisputable. An operative liberated it from one of their outposts. From an island between Siberia and Alaska."

"Perhaps it was planted."

"Big Diomede would be the last place anyone would plant anything."

"So why don't we just give Alaska back. In all the time since we purchased it in 1867, all we've gotten is oil at considerable environmental impact. And all the gold played out long ago."

"All played out on both counts, I'm afraid. And the Russians intend to claim the native peoples there originated from central Siberia."

"So, like the Crimea, they feel they need to protect all those indigenous Russians."

"That's pretty much it. That the last of those peoples arrived over 6,000 years before Russia came into existence doesn't seem to matter."

"Well, I've got worse problems."

"Care to share your priority list, Mister President?"

"Yes. A lesson in best of intentions. Not long ago, we encouraged the migration of people from Mexico and Central America. Even children. En masse. We knew two things. They would never be sent back, and they would someday all vote for us."

"The demographics at the time would bear that out."

"And then there are the laws of unintended consequences. Rather than going on welfare, as we had schemed, 80.4% of them finished school, mostly college, and entered the middle class."

"The American Dream."

"I'll thank you not to use that term again." The president relaxed his jaw. "In order to secure their newfound wealth, the ungrateful sons-of-bitches became Republicans."

"You can't trust anyone."

"We have to win, Cleveland. If the other party gets in, that American Dream will keep us out of power for the next 40 years."

"Sir, about Alaska?"

"Cleve, we're broke. Over $20,000,000,000,000 in debt. Twenty million millions. Do something for me. Calculate what our payment for Alaska in 1867 would be in today's dollars. Wait a minute. If it had been invested in the stock market—the S & P 500—all those years."

"You're considering selling Alaska?"

"Why not? Hell, they don't vote for us, anyway."

"You're right, there."

"We can make this work for us. I feel some delicious spin coming on."

"What do you want me to do?"

"For one, locate the operative who absconded with the intel so I can give him a medal."

CHAPTER 12

Still on Day 1, Kimbel sat alone opposite Editor Treadwell. It already felt like a long day, but the buttoned-up office provided the sensation that it would get even longer. And that he wouldn't be going home when the end-of-day whistle sounded.

"Today's Town Hall day. In San E, that means the elected elite lower themselves to speak to the great unwashed electorate. Since few of the electorate waste their time coming to the meetings, it'll be mostly press. Reporters such as yourself sift through obfuscating, Alan Greenspan-like political dialog for any words worth reporting. Since you are sworn to report the truth, you can only rely on words like 'the' and 'a' to have any scintilla of veracity. That's not really accurate. Politicians do report their stated projects, cost estimates, and expected completion dates, but all political numbers are random numbers generated by computers or drunks and serve no living purpose."

The new reporter stood, assuming the dialog to be complete. "I appreciate the preamble, Mr. Treadwell. I believe I can pick up the rest when I hear what they have to say and observe their body language." He turned to leave.

Treadwell cleared his throat.

Stones returned to his seat.

"So, enter Kimbel R. Stones," Treadwell intoned in majestic manner. "I'm hoping you've got the chops to inform the fine people of this Southern California time capsule as to what their elected officials are doing to screw them this time."

"It sounds like you are sending me on a quest," Stones said. "Would you like my report framed in such a way that the good people of San Ernestino make, as their next Home Depot purchases, copious amounts of tar and feathers?"

"We do reporting here, not vendettas or smears," Treadwell admonished. "We leave those to the TV networks and Internet blogs. You get me what I call the Sexy Six: the who, what, when, where, why, and how, and report it straight up." Treadwell added a rhetorical, "Do you understand?"

Stones mentally sorted out the Sexy Six, and nodded.

"We're not the *New York Times* or the *Washington Post* here. We don't look directly into some trusting reader's eyes and spin their head off. Think of it this way, have you ever served on a jury or watched an episode of Perry Mason?"

"With all due respect, I was too young for Perry Mason, but I have served on a few juries." Kimbel chuckled at the memories.

Treadwell knew there was more to the jury thing, but let it go.

"Tell the truth, the whole truth, and nothing but the truth, so help you God," Treadwell said, and then added with appropriate emphasis, "That translates into tell *only* the truth, give it *all* no matter how that might screw with your personal opinion, and don't supply anything that is extraneous or *not* true. Oh yes, and don't use bigger words than I do. Mine is the only private office, and I've had it since I started the paper." He finished the thought with his usual flair.

Stones canted his head to one side. "How about you? No wife?"

"Inquisitive is good," Treadwell noted. With that, he withdrew a well-polished .45 caliber Colt revolver from a drawer, laying it on his desk. "Point made?"

"Point made."

He replaced the antique weapon. "She left a newspaper hack—me—for a used-car salesman."

"A step down."

"She figured that out later."

"And the business at hand..."

"Yeah. Listen up. Here's a forewarning of what you'll see down there at City Hall. There are two drone-like council people, who are plug-compatible with Mayor Sallie Goddard. She's the one with the serious ambitions. She's the one to watch. But be careful. She smiles nice and does some serious positive damage to a lady's business suit, but she collects gonads by painful incision and doesn't recognize the word *enough*."

To keep from dozing, Kimbel inserted an incisive, "I see." into the editor's monologue.

The seasoned newsman continued unabated. "She's educated, some place back East, and she will look you straight in the eye and read every thought you've ever had. She's top notch in sizing up the competition, which is anyone but her. Don't try to BS the good mayor, or she'll chop up your aforementioned gonads and feed them to her piranhas. Then, she'll call me up and complain that her friggin' fish got an upset stomach from your remains."

"She's got piranhas?"

"Make fun all you want, new hire, but don't say I didn't warn you."

"Got it, boss," sucked up the new hire.

"Finally, I'm coming along just this first time, but if you see me talking to a cute blonde with legs that go clear up to her armpits, find your own way home. There are some things about the job that you'll learn later in your apprenticeship."

Silas Treadwell knew there was more to go, but he'd said enough for the time being. There would be additional talks.

CHAPTER 13

The drive downtown was not really necessary. The offices of the *Observer* were only six blocks away. Stones drove because Treadwell did not plan on coming back. In fact, he intended to score some time with the tricked-out blonde reporter from the *San Diego Union-Tribune*. The *Trib* was one of the two regionals and was, in fact, somewhat classier than the Los Angeles rag.

The BMW convertible, the one Stones had acquired at John Wayne Airport, exuded comfort and belied his lowly reporter status with the paper. It was clean inside; in fact, it had been recently detailed. Unknown to him, Treadwell contemplated a heart-to-heart discussion on the proper lifestyle of a small town reporter.

Besides Treadwell's number one motive of some serious face time with the blonde, his secondary reason for coming to one of the God-awful political rants was to hear and see what Kimbel saw and heard. That way, he could critique the reporting up front. It was important to set expectations early on with him. It forced him to pay attention to the political drivel this time, instead of his usual lust-filled daydreaming.

San Ernestino provided diagonal parking on the main street. The genius who brought that little upgrade to the already narrow street could no longer to be found. Treadwell considered congratulating him with a cattle prod enema. That's probably why he'd disappeared. Since the main street was crowned in the middle so rainwater would flow to the sides, when one parks diagonally, the passenger must attempt to exit the car by opening the door and holding it tightly so's it won't bang into the next car.

Treadwell had no more luck at it this time than in times past. Bang went the solid heavy door of the BMW. He thought out loud, "Oh look, it hit the mayor's car. Oh. What a shame."

He resisted the urge to hit it a few more times, closed the door, and led his new reporter into the building.

The City Hall building itself was exciting by San E standards. It had bay windows on the street level, regular business style windows on the second floor, and something unique: an ornate balcony in the middle of the second floor. The balcony protruded out over the sidewalk so elected servants could stand there with arms folded and look down on citizens, Mussolini-like. It was that kind of perk that caused a politician to spend several hundred thousand dollars on an election in order to secure a $90,000 per year job.

Inside, the building sported a '30s architecture with fish and scroll adornments made of imported cement. In Southern California, imported meant the workers were from Mexico.

Treadwell whispered toward Stones.

"Ceiling ornaments of a heavy material like cement are important so that they can take out the unwary in the event of our ever-impending earthquakes. It provides the building code version of natural selection."

Stones remarked, "The beige and cream tones lend the property its ambience. It embodies a special personal touch."

Cream was the natural color of Treadwell's skin, which darkened to beige after a modicum of beach time. He felt honored, and smiled.

It began well. They were seated by an usher who was appropriately deferential. He was different, as well.

Treadwell whispered to Kimbel. "The press generally receives seats with good visuals and good sound. The politicians are nice to us, not because of our lofty position as the Fourth Estate, but because they feel, if they can fool us, then we will go forth and fool their constituents. It saves them a lot of time and effort. Minimizing contact with the voting public is their highest priority."

The meeting was called to order and the mayor, characterized as honorable, was introduced. Mayor Sallie, as the press referred to her in private, wore what must have been a designer dress purchased at public expense along with appropriate hardware and requisite Prada shoes. She looked nice even with her pasted-on *I learned this in modeling school* smile.

During the mayor's carefully crafted speech, Treadwell noticed that Kimbel was taking copious notes. Once more, he whispered. "When Tram first started, he claimed he could remember everything—a photographic memory. I convinced him, using extensive logic followed by the threat of being fired, that all good reporters needed to take extensive notes in long-hand. That creates a permanent record should the reporter be chopped up and eaten by a crazed Managing Editor. Tram caught on quickly to the substance and mood of the explanation. Forever after he kept quite good notes."

The cute blonde reporter from the San Diego *Trib* asked what seemed to be a truly bonehead question after the narrative segment of the mayor's presentation. Treadwell nodded his head up and down and exclaimed to himself, "Right on! *Right on!*"

He glanced at Stones, whose eyes maintained the human equivalent of radar lock on the Mayor. Good enough. Less competition for the blonde.

When the question and answer session finished, Treadwell bade Stones a good evening and scooted over to the blonde's side. They got on well. After hearing that his ride had left without him, she offered to take him home. Hers.

CHAPTER 14

At NSA complex in Fort Meade, Maryland, the weather outside was not near as cold as the weather inside. Kimbel Stones' boss, Andrew Scott, did not like where the conversation with his own boss, Stanley Coin, was headed, and it hadn't even started.

"Sitrep on the Stones project, Andrew."

"Yes, Sir. He's not ready to come back voluntarily. Given the highest priority of the project, we could just grab him."

"He knows too much. Restrict him from travel with a passport watch."

"He'd still be a kidnap target."

"Well, if the CIA would just loan us their mind-screw drugs, we could erase his memories."

"So kidnappers would just grab him, torture him for information we'd erased, and then kill him."

The two mulled over the idea, but shook their heads in unison.

"Too drastic."

"We'd lose a good man, Sir."

"On the other hand, we could force him to return, but then we couldn't force him to think."

Both glanced over at the stained glass windows to observe rainwater that cascaded down. One found inspiration.

"I've got an idea, Andy my man. How about we help him with his personal situation? Last I checked, we do phone intercepts quite well."

"With this congress and president off-the-charts left, we could wind up in jail."

"We, Kemosabe?"

"I, Sir."

"See that you don't."

"Yes, Sir."

"I want a sitrep—a much more pleasing sitrep—on this in two."

"Two days. Yes, Sir." He turned to leave.

"One last item. Your annual review. I've scheduled it for next week."

Andrew left the room, wondering whether there really was a 1-800-Eat-Shit.

• • •

His interface with Andrew Scott complete, Stanley Coin left the National Security Agency's Fort Meade campus early. He'd contracted the unique NSA flu virus once again, he'd told his administrative assistant, and needed not to infect a major component of America's safety net.

In truth, he had a 9 P.M. call to make. The time zone for that call was five hours to the east of Fort Meade. The recipient was likely the most powerful man on Earth.

South on 97 took him to Annapolis, then east across the Chesapeake Bay on 14. Normal was Highway 50 home. Not today.

He crossed the Delaware state line a half hour later and, as if on automatic, turned south into the parking lot for the Harrington

Raceway And Casino. He passed a marquee for a Herman's Hermits concert with a likeness of a smiling, fair-haired Peter Noone peering down at him. Stanley allowed that he'd once looked that carefree and happy.

He slapped on a visor supported by a thick headband. He plugged a dangling earpiece into his right ear. The amazing nano-technology, directional radar components arrayed inside would alert him whenever someone approached.

In the casino, he found his usual corner. The hubbub of a couple hundred would-be winners accompanied by the siren song of just as many slot machines proved better than a hotel room with the radio turned up.

Assured he sat in acoustic isolation, Stanley utilized a special phone—voice disguised with digital packets employing multiple encryptions federated over multiple satellites. On pick up, he relayed his own sitrep. He listened. "Yes, Elder."

• • •

Twelve minutes and twenty-seven seconds later, Stanley Coin heard with relief the 'click' on the other end. The ultimate boss appeared to have received the situation report well, but was perceptibly concerned with the inability of Coin to control his subordinate once removed, Kimbel Stones. In fact, the Elder seemed impressed with Stones' aptitude *and* attitude—two necessary components for success.

No time for a little Omaha High-Low in the Harrington's popular Poker Room, Stanley headed out and tried not to worry for his own well-being as he headed south on 13 to his hometown. He smiled. Delmar Delaware and Delmar Maryland seemed to be one and the same. In fact, the motto "The Little Town Too Big For One State" put the burg square on the state line.

Partly a release of tension, he laughed at his experiences with the states' taxing authorities. Both had visited him, demanding he pay taxes in their respective jurisdictions. Of course, he'd seated each of them on the side of his home that resided in the other state, so that anything he said or promised was invalid.

And there he was. Both and neither. On the payroll of the NSA, as well as the Elder's ultra-secret Illuminé organization, and trying to keep himself out of a federal prison for treason, or worse, from turning into one of the Elder's cleansings. Dead.

CHAPTER 15

The next day began the way they always did in coastal Southern California. Seventy-two degrees Fahrenheit, partly-cloudy, and so forth. Traffic remained light since the largest portion of inhabitants—the tourists—were not up and about at 6:30 A.M.

Treadwell sauntered, swaggered actually, into the office a little late and with an uncharacteristic smile.

Susanna, already in, observed, "Lookie who got laid last night." She often made it clear that marketing types were neither shy nor retiring.

Treadwell ignored her, trod his way past the City Desk into his office, and sank into the sumptuous leather chair he referred to as his throne. He had left the door open on purpose and called out to Susanna, "Hey, Soooosie Poo. How about getting me a nice hot cup of java?"

"Blankety-blank... and the horse you rode in on, Sir," she replied, vainly attempting to sound respectful.

Blown back to reality, he stood, stepped over to the Keurig, and fixed some coffee. French Roast. Black.

Back at his desk, he summoned the new reporter of political platitudes over the intercom, "Hey, Kimbel. When you have a moment, I want to see you in my office. That means now!" he shouted.

Kimbel loped in, papers in hand. He dropped several pages of printer output on the editor's desk and waited, possibly, for some gratitude.

"Dismissed," said the old man, not even looking up.

When Stones performed an about face and left the office, Treadwell began to read his first article on the most overhyped and unworthy topic of all—politics. It was good. No, it was very good. No, it was excellent. The new-hire provided the Sexy Six in terse and intensely accurate prose. Treadwell mentally applied the appropriate grade for his first epistle by exclaiming, "*Fucking A!*"

He called his reporter back in to congratulate him, but thought better of it. He might want a raise. "Here. Take this to Luisa for proofreading. And don't ask her if her name is Spanish, it's Portuguese. Born in some place called Sintra. The most romantic spot in all Portugal, she told me."

Stones left and returned after a too-brief time.

"What did I hire, the modern version of a bad penny?"

Stones neither spoke nor left.

"What is it?" Treadwell asked.

"That was fun. What's next?"

"Since we don't allow masturbation on company time, why don't you go help Luisa proof the *good* stories.

"*Good* stories?"

"They're the once-a-day wire stories plus those we cop from the Internet. Oh yes, and Tram's stuff. Oh, and no incest, either. Proofing your own material is a no-no."

Stones left.

Treadwell faced a positive reality. His new reporter's story was not just good, it was great. With that, the editor realized he had this morning learned two important lessons. One, he had made an exceptionally good hire, relying totally on his instincts and, two, he definitely could not afford this guy.

But he quite unknowingly had made two near fatal errors. He hadn't advised him to find a job worthy of his talents, and he'd sent him in to spend time with Luisa. Big mistake, that last one.

CHAPTER 16

Stones introduced himself again to Luisa and asked if he could help. She appeared quite busy. He expected her to say, "No, thanks." Then, he would be on his way to research the mayor. Instead, she stopped proofing whatever story was in front of her and rocked back in her seat. She looked him over, but most of her time was spent looking into his eyes. She opened her mouth a little, clicking the tail end of her pencil on her teeth.

He reckoned that the popular misconception about Luisa was that everything she did seemed to be calculated to reach inside a man, tear the power to resist from his body, and flush it to where such manly powers went to die. Stones' conclusion: that was not the case. He convinced himself that it was all natural behavior for Luisa. What you saw was what you got. Or wished you got.

With red ink squiggles and cryptic edits, she proofed each story, and sent it, via the copy boy, back to the author. Since the paper had only one reporter in the past, that was always Tram. When she got to Kimbel's story, she read it and she liked it. There were a couple of items to flag, but even they were subjective catches.

"So, what do you do when you aren't covering big stories?" she asked.

"I spend a lot of time with family—with a couple I've known, it seems, forever. They were friends of my parents."

"Were?"

"Yeah, my parents died when I was a kid. No one ever determined who was responsible."

Her interest piqued, Luisa's expression intensified.

He almost added that he'd utilized all the resources of the NSA, but still no luck with respect to his parents' deaths. He swallowed that disclosure, bypassed her inquisition, and moved on.

"The Hans took me in before the Child Services people could get their hands on me. They saved me from an orphanage. I learned to love and respect them as I had my parents. Now, they're in their latter years and the current hard times are particularly hard on them. I took a leave to come take care of them." He knew he'd left out the sordid details. He hoped she wouldn't pry.

She looked at him as only a woman can look when it comes to relationship issues. "So what did you do for work that you could just pick up and head west? How could you do such a thing?"

"It was just a government job back in D.C. Nothing important enough to talk about."

Her eyes lingered.

She let it drop.

She handed him his marked-up copy and watched him walk out of her cozy. This was going to be interesting, she thought to herself.

CHAPTER 17

The American president came into office just like his predecessors. He'd had the drapes changed. He'd had the oval rug changed. He'd chosen the Resolute Desk as had six presidents before. But it was more for him. Obsessive Compulsive Disorder plus the added benefit of clinical paranoia. The drapes and rug were gone, because he worried that they might contain nano listening devices. Or fiber-optic video surveillance capability.

The desk and the requisite portraits of Washington and Lincoln had been examined for bugs by disparate members of the Executive Branch with the president assembling and comparing their findings. Those sorts of things normally persecuted him. Then, there was the job.

It wasn't the state of domestic issues that bothered him. That would muddle along. It wasn't the condition of foreign affairs, either. He didn't care a nit about what went on beyond America's borders. After all, foreigners didn't get to vote.

No, it was the damn walls. Why were they not square like everywhere else? Conformity was the key to life.

His chief-of-staff knocked politely, then entered. He glanced at a painting. "We'll have to take that picture down."

"That's one of my heroes. Norman Mattoon Thomas. He stood up for fair treatment of the poor way back in the 30's. And the lower classes."

The chief-of-staff knew that the president possessed no knowledge with regard to the poor and lower classes, having been a trust fund baby. He kept his disgust to himself. "When the cameras come in, as they do from time-to-time, they'll catch that, and the evil cable news bunch will run with it."

"Let 'em. I'll give a little speech showing that they are champions of the oppressors."

"Like oil companies."

"Yes."

"We just received a very nice contribution…"

The president grimaced. "Why do we have to whore out?"

"Because, with all due respect, Mr. President, we are whores."

"I want to change the walls, make 'em square."

"Change the Oval Office into the Square Office? I don't think that's a good idea. Besides, we'd lose the alliteration."

"Great. Now I have to concern myself with grammar embellishments, on top of everything else."

"Before we worry about the walls, there's the Alaska issue."

"Remind me."

"The Russian ambassador is still waiting. He wants to conclude the deal. Oh, and we'll need *our* ambassador to Russia present."

"Abigail," the president called.

A red-head with freckles everywhere stepped from the bathroom. "Yes?"

"Please change out of my robe. The Russian is here."

She winked at the COS. "Fifteen minutes." She stepped out of view.

• • •

Fifteen minutes to the second later and the Russian, along with his translator, was escorted into the Oval Office. The president remained seated at his desk. He barely smiled as he nodded the man into a sumptuous chair opposite.

"So, Mr. Ambassador, what is this deal you wished to discuss?"

"It is simple and equitable. The American Secretary of State Seward paid $7.9 million to Russia for the Alaska territory in 1867. We will pay the equivalent of $7.9 million now."

"You mean adjusted for inflation."

"We will pay the equivalent in Russian rubles."

The president chuckled. "That, and your mama giving me head, and we have a deal."

The translator translated.

The Russian glared.

"Adjusted for the inflation average for just over 150 years…" Abigail quickly tapped sparkling pink nails on her Smartphone. "…that $7.9 million is worth $127 million in today's dollars."

"That would merely reflect the degradation of your currency," countered the Russian.

"And you want to pay us in rubles?"

The president produced a quite serious laugh.

"Uh, we've had some misfortune with our money."

"From communism to mafia-ism." The president smiled. "Let's discuss a figure in the middle, payment in dollars, and a promise to stay out of the ANWAR with your oil drilling."

The Russian lifted his chin.

The president leaned forward, speaking in a whisper. "It goes down like this. Unofficially, you will pay $20,000,000 each for my ambassador to your fine country and my chief-of-staff." He motioned the two dumbstruck, referenced individuals out of the room. When they closed the door, he spoke even more softly. "And for me…"

CHAPTER 18

A day had passed since the mayor's meeting with what she'd referred to as the plebeian masses. Born to a well-to-do family, she viewed her mayoral status as more of a birthright than a selection of the plebes.

Sallie Goddard reviewed her calendar and sat back with a sigh. Politicians could lie, but they couldn't outsmart the date-certain in November. She and the rest of the political elite would have to stop business as usual for a month and get re-elected. Actually, it was not quite that simple.

In San Ernestino, the Council of the Mayor consisted of a mayor plus two council persons. Every two years, the mayor's job shifted to one of the other council members. So every six years, Sallie cycled back into the mayor's slot.

The stakeholders in this cozy arrangement were three in number. First, there were the elected representatives of the people. They held the power simply because they held the purse strings and made the rules.

Second came the business types, not the least of which were real estate developers. As major contributors in several ways, they kept the good times rolling. And rolling. And rolling some more. She smiled at that one.

Last of the three were the fine citizens of San Ernestino. They just rolled along—having little or no political interests or aspirations—doing whatever they did for living and loving, and paying little heed to the local government. They paid even less attention to the state or federal governments. Had Sallie Goddard ever compared them to an animal, she would have called them sheep.

Her dream state musings were interrupted by a quickly opened door, and the hastened emergence of her number one assistant and confidant.

Sallie looked up, carrying the previous thoughts forward.

"I could put my speeches on CD and just replay them. As news, this place is a snoozer. I'd be front page. Above the fold, as they say."

"We'll have to discuss the electioneering later."

"Very well. Take a seat."

"Yes, ma'am."

"So what is it that can't wait today?" she asked the young man seated across from her.

"It's McCracken. He wants that tract next to the wetlands. Above the cliffs. Says he can put forty condos there and not disturb the little fuckers," said Willie Sample, her lieutenant in crime.

"Remind me," said the mayor. "Who are the 'little fuckers'?"

"You know. The bugs and frogs and stuff that those assholes in Sacramento are always trying to protect. A little toxic this and that would get rid of the problem, but I would have to violate most environmental laws to get it done. May I have your approval?"

"That's real funny. We have a good thing going and don't need those state crapheads in our face about anything, let alone a bunch of 'little fuckers.' What else does McCracken need us for?"

"Seems there is one house in the way of his current bluff-top project. Old couple been living there for years. McCracken needs the property. End of story."

"What end of story? Does he think we can just apply eminent domain on some whim that popped out of his ass? Why can't we get along without him? We get to be mayor again every four years and it's status quo in between. What's not to like? Why do we need this asshole? We've got economic and social lockdown on good old Saint Ernie."

"Sallie." He paused a second. "Ms. Mayor. We have a local government trend in motion and the only thing we really know about trends is that, at some point, they stop. McCracken has done a couple of material off-the-books tasks for us."

"So. Big Deal." She paused to distance herself, should they be bugged, from the answer she knew too well. "To what manner of tasks do you refer?"

"The kind of tasks for which people can spend a number of years looking at the world through fixed steel vertical blinds. Dig?"

"I'm not sure of which you speak, but I am sure that I … what was the term? … ah, yes. Dig."

Willie noticed the change in the mayor's demeanor. It occurred every time McCracken's name came up. "I swept your office and my ante-room for bugs just an hour ago. We're clean. So let's talk straight."

He produced an 'okay?' nod.

She responded in kind.

He continued.

"We have to work with him on this one. Then he'll go away until the next time he feels the need to extort political power from us."

"What about this old couple? Can't we have them declared incompetent and put them in a home. You know, show a little empathy," said the mayor in a sincere-sounding tone.

Willie just rolled his eyes.

"Alright. Check with our attorney on the eminent domain thing. It would be hell to pay if a couple of geezers stood in the way of progress," said Sallie, while rubbing the tips of her thumb and first two fingers together.

Sample felt like a computer type saying 'we're in' to a successful password breach.

"And let McCracken know that we're on it, okay?"

"That's always easy seeing as how we share the same attorney. He can update our favorite asshole developer, client privilege and all," observed Willie.

"Now, if there's nothing else, please get the fuck out of my office."

Lieutenant Sample promptly spun around on his immaculately polished shoes and headed back to his lesser digs.

The mayor pushed back, picked up her prized coffee mug she'd acquired in San E's Russian sister city, sipped the very high-end Rémy Martin X.O. cognac, and stepped to her side window. Corruption wasn't all it was cracked up to be. Whoring herself and her town out to special interests, unlike male effluent, left a bad taste in her mouth. If it wasn't for the perqs. She smiled. The perqs were so wonderful, she thought of them while pleasuring herself to sleep each night.

She closed her eyes. Her fingers began to wander. Taking another glance, she sipped the cognac and peered out at her very own little town.

Yes. The perqs.

CHAPTER 19

The Hans did not live in a fancy place. It was a 50's era three bedroom, one bath on a quiet street that ran along the top of the bluffs. Quiet until McCracken and company began to pursue their lot. The Hans had heard about John McCracken. While he was always introduced formally as Mr. John McCracken of John McCracken Developers, Inc., the locals just called him 'Porky.'

And with good reason. Not only did the term accurately describe the extended girth of the man, but it also characterized correctly his tight relationship with City Hall. There are not a lot of restaurants in San Ernestino and it was not infrequent that McCracken and the mayor were seen having lunch or dinner or drinks, no doubt at the townspeople's expense. A gathering storm in San E, currently just a mumble, might grow to a shout before long.

Everybody liked the Hans. The mister was in his early 70's, but at a stocky five-foot-seven, he still possessed the strength and demeanor of a wise old mentor of Korean heritage. His wife, born in Pusan, Korea, had moved to the American East Coast with him 58 years ago.

They had relocated to San Ernestino when Quentin had retired from government service in Washington, D.C.

After Kimbel's second day at the paper—about seven o'clock—he came strolling into the house with a smile.

"Good evening," he said in flawless Korean.

He had known the Hans for quite some time, before and after his parents died. Quentin had served in the Korean Marine Corps in Vietnam with Kimbel's father. During a vicious firefight with the Viet Cong, his father had saved Quentin's life. To most Asians, such an act obliges the saved party with a lifelong obligation. It was one that Kimbel's dad did not call in or even mention. Still, it was there.

Kimbel walked into the den.

On the wall were plaques containing a variety of Quentin's accomplishments. One plaque contained the formal acknowledgement of his 8th degree Black Belt standing in the Korean martial art known as Tang Soo Do. Also, there was a framed copy of his promotion to sergeant in the Korean Marine Corps.

Kimbel knew the full meaning of that military entity. His father had told him that, whenever there was some choice as to whom to fight or to whom to surrender, the enemy always chose anyone other than the Koreans. They were known worldwide as one of the most disciplined and toughest fighting forces ever to take the field of battle.

"I see you have found my modest accomplishments," said Quentin, who stood behind Stones. "It is not a lot for a lifetime."

Stones spoke without turning, "There are plenty of people with walls full of pointless awards. These I see here have meaning that is far beyond the framed paper. My dad always did whatever had to be done. No matter what the risk. You are like him in that respect."

Quentin was far too humble to respond. Stones had moved to the bookshelves lining the walls. The bookshelves were full of the classic tales. Each represented in both English and Korean versions.

"I use the English versions to help me with your most difficult language. I guess I should say our language, since I have been a citizen for over forty years. I am a synthesis of cultures, Kimbel. I love the country of my birth and will go out of my way for good Kimchi. But I have been enamored by American culture since I was small. Did you know? My favorite TV show was your Route 66 with Glenn Corbett and Martin Milner. It was delivered to us with Korean dubbing. I wanted so much to believe that the stars knew both languages. Please, come with me," Quentin said as he opened the door to the garage.

Kimbel followed him out the door. Kimbel first saw the Han family car but then, as he turned to his left, he saw what Quentin wanted to show. It was a sports car with white inserts in the door panels. A 1960 light blue Corvette that he concluded was an exact duplicate of the Route 66 car. As he stepped over to it, he could see that it was in immaculate condition. There was no top, which accentuated the free spirit nature the TV series had so typified.

"Quentin, I can just picture Glen Corbett and George Maharis."

"It was Martin Milner, as Tod Stiles, and Maharis as Buz Murdoch."

That brought a smile. "Whoa, there. You know your stuff, Quentin."

Han relaxed. He smiled back. "When Maharis got sick, he was replaced by Glenn Corbett, as Lincoln Case. Right?"

"Right enough. C'mon. All this guy talk is leaving one very important person out. Bettie."

"Guy talk? She knows this stuff better than I do."

They went back inside and into the living room.

"We were just talking about the Route 66 show," Stones threw at the kitchen doorway.

"Did you know, Corbett was born Glenn Edwin Rothenburg? Before acting, he served in the U.S. Navy as a Seabee? From CB as in Construction Battalion."

Both men nodded agreement. Bettie was data-wise down with the series.

As they settled on the couch, she walked in carrying a tea service. For a woman to serve the men tea was tradition. Bettie carried out her traditional role with pride. But Kimbel could see that there was significant effort and some pain on her part. When she left, he turned to Quentin, who poured the tea.

"There is a problem?" he asked.

"Yes. But we plan a long road trip after she has had her operation. She will recuperate and then we will take the Corvette." Quentin beamed as he looked across Kimbel toward the kitchen. "We will retrace the path of the historic Route 66. Just like on TV," he added wistfully.

Kimbel watched him. He knew that Bettie would be fine and the Hans would make that trek. They would have their dream.

Just then, the mood was broken by the door chime. Quentin got up from the couch and answered it. He came back into the living room, leading a young man. The man introduced himself to them as Mark Smithson. He announced he was on official business from the Mayor's office, but that it was nothing too serious. He asked if Mrs. Han could be present and then proceeded to pass on what had to be someone else's message.

"I have been told, Mr. and Mrs. Han, that you have lived here for many years. We respect that, and would want nothing better than for you to live out your years in harmony and pleasantness."

Quentin and Bettie listened intently, trying to figure out what this was all about. Was the mayor's office going around wishing everyone well? Of course, an election was coming up. Maybe that was it. But Kimbel detected Mr. Smithson's opening words portended that this discussion would soon go south.

Smithson got right to the point. "As you know, San Ernestino is more than any one citizen. Or any one of our fine families. It is a community. And sometimes, what is best for one or two families must subordinate to what is best for the whole."

Here it comes, thought Kimbel, recognizing salesman talk for what it was. He thought about picking this guy up, taking him out back, and tossing him over the cliff. Kimbel's solution for dealing with all salesmen. He did not suffer them well. But no, this is not

Washington, D.C. He should reserve final judgment. For maybe another five minutes.

"Now this land along the bluff where your house is located is prime property and we wouldn't want you to lose it or anything, but, as you can see, there are a number of undeveloped acres on either side of you. The council has concluded that this entire property could become of tremendous value to the city and, of course, to *all* of its citizens, if you would just reconsider your decision not to sell this last remaining property. You would be doing a tremendous service to your fellow townspeople. And to the future of San Ernestino. Can you see that?" he asked in his best plaintive voice.

"Mr. Smithson," Quentin began. "Thank you for personally delivering your message to us. We have already told the developer's emissaries 'no' on a number of occasions. We absolutely love our home here, and we plan to stay here until we have both finished our time on this Earth. Our position has not changed, and I do not expect it to change. So, please, tell the mayor for us that we respect our community and all of its members. All we ask is for everyone to respect our choice, as well."

"But, if I could just have a few more minutes, I'm sure..."

His salesman-like 'don't take no for an answer' repartee was interrupted when Stones stood. "Thank you, Mr. Smithson, I believe we are done now. I'll show you out." He thought 'throw you out' would be more appropriate.

Kimbel indicated with a sweep of his arm the path Mark Smithson should take. The path led to the front door and beyond.

When Smithson had left, the three of them brushed off the latest attempt to persuade the Hans to sell their property. Stones still didn't think throwing Smithson over the bluff was a bad idea, but he let it slide. He did not know it now, but he would revisit the notion of extreme prejudice at a later date.

CHAPTER 20

A week had gone by. The warm Santa Ana winds flowing from the California, Nevada, and Arizona deserts were coming to an end. It was time for autumn to begin, or at least appear so. There just would not be any turning of the leaves. The Southern California coast does not do that natural phenomenon well at all.

Kimbel had just dropped off another 'local politics' piece for proofreading and already Luisa the Proofreader was causing him to take notice. Silas was right. She made no effort to be sexual, but even her not trying was sexually profound. Still, he needed to stay focused. One had to strut one's stuff in the beginning of any job just to put an exclamation after the 'good hire' notion every boss puts on hold right after the new hire begins work.

As Kimbel passed the advertising department, the normally effusive Susanna looked up from an ad she was composing and effused, "Hey, you gonna ask the required question or not? Like 'where's a guy go to get a bite to eat around here?' " Her sly smile added that this was not the simple question it seemed.

"Alright. It's lunch time. Where's a guy... et cetera," he asked as if it was his idea. He decided to understand the game, and then determine the rules.

"Ah. He wants to play. Time to engage the enemy," she thought out loud. "If you are looking for Mexican food, there's Gilberto's Hispanic three blocks down. It's a chain owned by the governor, but no matter. Great food at newspaper employee prices. It's buffet—you can eat as much as you like." Another sly look. He understood that Little Miss Inuendo was not talking food.

"And if I don't like Hispanic food, there's..." he asked playfully.

"Well, if you really want something more exotic like sushi, pheasant, Kobe beef and like that, there's... ta-da... Gilberto's."

Her vibrant green eyes laser-locked on Kimbel's blue counterparts the whole time. Her expression displayed the 'I'm funny *and* a beautiful blonde babe' effect she wanted to portray. "It's an inexpensive date and my millionaire lunch just cancelled, damn the luck. Bend over and grab your wallet. We need to get this done before it snows again."

"What is this wallet grabbing? Whatever happened to Dutch treat?"

"Honey," she started into a passable Aretha Franklin impression, "the only other thing you goin' be axed to grab at a small-town rag are yo' ankles."

It was a hard sell with her straight blonde hair and fair skin. Wearing a cream, fitted pant suit, a designer silk scarf, and red flats, Susanna looked more like a high-class cover girl than a sassy woman from the 'hood.

"Okay, okay." He laughed. "I'll buy if you promise not to do anymore ethnic impressions."

"Deal," she said. She apprehended her Coach bag, and they headed off to Gilberto's.

• • •

Gilberto's had its normal lunch crowd. They easily found a table. Kimbel could already smell the *refritos* and *arroz* cooking in the back.

He had noticed the public health sign on the way in and was not too sure about this place.

"It's okay, Jose," Susanna said. "A big red 'C' instead of a blue 'A' or 'B' just means the Mexican food is great. Just like Tijuana. If the cockroaches are over three inches, then Public Health gives out a red 'D'. Hell, *they* eat here all the time."

Kimbel was up for gamesmanship today. He felt good. The Hans were doing fine. So, game on.

"Susanna, I think I'm in love with you already, so tell me, which one of you two women…" He referenced Luisa. "…is the office gossip? Hmmm? I am just dying to know who is doing what to whom, and I'm hoping you're the right girl."

"Gossip?" she said. "Girl?" she said. She tried to look offended, but quickly gave up. "Okay. The old man used to work for a paper up north of Los Angeles. Oxnard. He put in a lot of years working up from copy boy to reporter to city editor. He told me all about it. He has some great memories. I mean, wire service stories used to come in on punched paper tape, for Chrissakes. I think even the Romans were more modern than that. He would sort the tapes and then fetch them when the City Desk crew picked out the wire stories they wanted to run."

"What did he do with the tapes?"

"He'd run the appropriate tapes into the back room for the linotype operators to load. The reporters would throw in local crap, the ad girl would throw in the ads, then the classifieds, obituaries, TV guides, and poof, a paper was made. They used school kids to make afternoon deliveries. It all worked out until the early '90's. The union came in, promised everyone to double their pay. Who could pass that up? But employees' salaries being the number one expense item, three years later the paper went belly up. He moved down here. Tried some other jobs, saved up some cash, and started the *Observer*. He knows the business from a small-town perspective.

"Next, there's the proof girl. You probably didn't notice her, but the boss has the hots for her. You can tell when he's thinking about her 'cause that's when he drools. Some day, he'll drool all the time. But it's just for Luisa now. Anyway, I'm sure she's got sexually transmitted diseases—the incurable ones—so I'd stay away if I were you."

"It seems," he said, "my job requires me to help with the proofing whenever the load ramps up. However, I do appreciate the altruistic advice. I'll try to make sure she and I don't have sex."

Susanna sat back.

Kimbel watched her think.

She stared at nothing in particular.

He continued to watch her think.

The little bitch had already planted her demon seed. Susanna must work fast, she thought. Kimbel was one good looking dude and, as foxy as she knew she was, her biological clock was picking up speed. She needed to hook up with a good one before she turned thirty next year.

Susanna went on with dossiers on Tram and the others, but she could tell that Kimbel was still thinking Luisa. "So, there you have it. How about you?" she asked.

"You skipped one. Susanna Thomson," he parried.

"Me? I started growing up in Florida. Key West itself. I was doing the Duval Crawl before I was 18. My memories of Key West's main drag and the 'severality' of the bars are a bit of a blur. I moved out to LA to become a star actress, singer, et cetera. Did some college at USC on my old man's dime and my marketing major with communications concentration brought me to San Ernestino—marketing capital of the world."

"And your mother?"

"I thought you'd guess. I do dress a little upscale for San E. My mom was a model. New York, no less. She taught me how to dress and apply makeup before I hit puberty. Drove the boys wild."

Kimbel knew a partial story when he heard one. There was much more to know about this interesting young woman. Also time for a new subject. "Mr. Treadwell, Silas, has me reporting the local political scene. What do you know about the mayor?"

"She is not only THE political scene, she is the fashion scene, the power scene, and all else."

"Whoa," Kimbel stopped her short. "What power? This town has barely enough people to have electrical power, let alone political power. Is there more to this place than meets the eye?" he asked.

For the first time, Susanna seemed uncomfortable. She glanced around to see if anyone was listening, and then leaned closer to Kimbel.

He smelled a delicate but persistent scent he'd missed at the office. It seemed that the lady had left the office prepared to go on offense. This was not a good time to lose focus. But it had been a long time. Like any good reporter, he pursued what was known in newspaper circles as *The Dirt.*

"Ms. Goddard has got this place locked up, Kimbel. The big real estate developer is fronting all of her 'Hey, look at me' money. She gets elected by a landslide every time she runs. Guess that's because any opponents seem to get discouraged prior to election time. But mark my words, there's an undercurrent in good ole San E that's going to jump up and bite her in her well worn ass someday. It's just waiting for the right man to come along. A leader, you know what I mean? This is a retired-person and service-person community like a lot of the small beach towns. Leaders don't show up but every 300 to 400 years."

"Excellent. If you don't mind, I'd like to keep our conversations confidential. Just between us. Is that alright?"

He observed the effect of his intimation of intimacy in her eyes. She smiled her response.

They finished up at Gilberto's and returned to the paper in the allotted half-hour. Kimbel was starting to get some sizzle to go with the flavor. He planned to keep a good relationship with new informant Susanna. She knew and she talked—a good combination.

CHAPTER 21

At the end of the work day, Stones dialed Susanna's number and asked about dinner. Her first notion was to thank him, but say no. He intrigued. She acquiesced. After all, he was a reporter, and she needed to keep her own backstory under wraps.

Not wanting to chance Gilberto's Hispanic twice in one day, they headed a short distance north of San Ernestino to the local surfer's paradise, Ventria, and its 50's style diner.

As they approached, they were greeted by the front half of a '56 Cadillac convertible, filled with flowers and shrubs. It appeared to be a perfect mood setter for the place.

Inside, the rear half poked through the wall, and finished the thought. A pair of rambunctious two-year-olds climbed over the trunk and bounced on the back seat.

"You ever been in a back seat?" she teased.

"It was a different bounce."

Their host, reminiscent of a mid-life Elvis Presley, walked them to an empty booth to the strains of Bobby Day's Rockin' Robin.

Stones and Susanna glanced at menus, ate, and then just peered into each other's eyes. Each of them realized they'd moved beyond mere public conversations. Few additional words were spoken.

Two hours later, they sat naked on a bed in the adjacent Motel 6. Stones peered down at the paisley-patterned carpet that hadn't suffered the bane of vacuuming for quite some time. He spoke first.

"Some serious talk, okay?"

She usually saw things coming. But, this. Not this soon. She turned to watch his eyes as he continued.

"I've been places, Susanna."

"We all have."

"Places I've never been."

"That's easy to process."

"What I mean—"

"You have been to places you've never been to. Let me get out my LSD. Some serious sugar cubes. Three? No, four."

She stared into a corner of the room, then returned her gaze to him. "How can I have a relationship with a man whose picture sits in the dictionary next to the word *enigma*? Hmmm?" She pursed her lips. "Enigma Stones. I like that."

"It means I can't go very far with a woman. Any woman."

"Did you just throw cold water on us?"

"I'm sorry."

"No problem. Was the sex we just had okay? Where you placed your hand on my heart? To feel the heat and passion I have for you? Was it okay?"

He'd not seen her angry. Always calm and collected. "It's just that I fear we won't be able to get close. Necessarily close."

Susanna stiffened her jaw, as she'd done over the years, to hold back the emotions. It didn't work. Several drops cascaded over her perfect cheeks.

"There's some backstory here, isn't there?" The empathy showed on Stones' face as he leaned back. Giving her space. "I'm sorry to have provoked whatever it is. You can trust me ... and that's what all of this is about. Between us."

She laughed slightly, then snatched a tissue from an end-table. "No one's made my makeup run before."

"Here. Let me make it up to you." He started toward her.

She threw up her hands in mock objection. "Don't touch me."

Slowly, he extended a finger. "Just here."

She reacted to the touch with a moan.

"And here ..."

CHAPTER 22

Kimbel Stones and Susanna Thomson moved to the bed and made love the slow way. The one that exuded the deep trust to which Stones had alluded. They'd stepped into a new world. In a Motel 6. In the aftermath, it was he who answered the unasked. Backstory.

"I work for a government agency located in Maryland. It gathers information. Sorts it. Makes sense of it."

"National security, I'm guessing."

"They sent me to an island. Off the Alaska coast. To pick something up."

"The island?"

"One of the two Diomede islands. The big one."

"Dangerous?"

"Something like that. A man from another agency had to brave an Arctic blizzard to save my ass. Or I wouldn't be here."

"Then I should thank him. How was it he was even there?"

"I was told that the *Company* had a man in the area, collecting intel, of course."

"The CIA."

He rolled right, facing her. "Company equals CIA. How do you know that?"

"I read spy thrillers. C'mon. Give."

"Give what?"

"Did he have a name?"

"Always the news woman."

"Advertising."

"I was only provided his code name."

"Which was?"

Stones chuckled at her persistence. "They referred to him as Magic Man."

"From what you've told me, he was definitely that."

"Saved my bacon."

She slid her hand over his thigh. "And the rest."

"I shouldn't mention the woman."

"Another woman? That excites me." She moved her head down to his belly.

"A young FBI Agent."

"Did you know her? In the biblical sense?"

"Funny you should put it that way. She did yell out '*Oh, God!*' a couple of times. Our first, and only, time was in a church. A meet. A secret room upstairs behind the organ tubes."

"Mmm. Organ tube."

Susanna moved lower.

His breathing ramped to that reminiscent of his stress event on Big Diomede.

"Dogs barking in the hunt. Shots fired wildly in the white out."

"Were you hit?"

"Just once. I guess it's obvious it wasn't fatal."

In the next instant, the FBI agent's countenance flashed in his mind. Another blonde. Athletic. The 'neighbor' girl. Completely different from Susanna.

"There was someone else. A woman. One tough piece of gingerbread."

"I've heard about your fetish. The gingerbread."

He'd only told Luisa about that. He had to be more careful. He wished to Hell that FBI Agent Phoebe Bransfield was here to help with this mess.

"There's more, isn't there?"

"It's complicated."

"You've only got 47 seconds left."

"The Fibbee was supposed to be there … to protect me once I got back to Little Diomede. Back from the Russian one. Got stuck west of Nome, her take off point on the Alaska coast, due to the weather. The CIA jumped-in its asset and got me out of there. They're holding a chit with the FBI for that, just waiting to cash it in. Sometime in the future, Phoebe will have some non-Bureau work to do. Dangerous work."

She looked up, but kept her hands busy. "I heard the CIA types can't perform operations in the U.S. They could get … Phoebe … to do something, huh?"

"Yeah. They could get her to do something."

CHAPTER 23

Life continued on at the *Observer* for several more weeks. Kimbel learned the drill of taking good notes at City Hall meetings and laid down a great story. He had Silas Treadwell's six 'W's down pat, and letters to the editor began to pour in, proclaiming him the next Mark Twain. It made the previous political reporter, Treadwell, look like he should throw in the towel and retire to reporter boot hill. Fortunately, he had the editor and owner—himself—to fall back on.

Silas recalled that he'd been fat, dumb, and happy until Kimbel started breezing into his office frequently to chat about local politics. The mystery man from the East Coast started referring to the 'Stepford' Mayor and her pasted-on smile. And then, Silas got the call from Mayor Sallie, herself.

"Hi, there, Silas. How are you today? I am sure you are fine, and I am fine, as well."

Eyes closed, the editor envisioned the signature pasted-on smile she'd applied prior to making the call.

"I have kind of gotten to know your new reporter, what's his name, ah, yes, Kimbel Stones. He does a pretty good job. I don't have a single complaint. I wanted you to understand *this* isn't *that* kind of call." She said it in a way that told him *here comes the other shoe.*

She continued. "You're aware that there will be another election in November, I'm sure, and... you are aware, aren't you?"

"Yes. I've been here for a long time, and we have these things now and then." Once again, she treated him like one of the morons who worked for her. For some reason, the term bitch-slap came to mind. "Go on." Finish, he silently begged.

"First of all, an observation. Silas, your paradigm is out-of-date. Nowadays, television networks support incumbents with whom they agree. They toss negative stories and embellish positive ones.

"That's not journalism."

"No, but everybody wins. Businesses and people considering relocation drop the idea when they see negativity regarding a town. They head for places with good newspaper PR. And low crime. That's all I'm suggesting."

Treadwell knew that Sheriff Connor was on board with maintaining low-crime statistics. He also knew the man merely moved the criminals elsewhere.

"You were saying about my new reporter..."

"It would serve purpose if Mister Kimbel would just give the present administration, which would be mine, a little positive nod between now and then. I am sure that some of my better-to-do supporters would be willing to throw some extra ad space your way." Her voice trailed up at the end as if to imply a question.

"Ow!" he cried out. He'd managed to pick up and gore himself with the Hirohito Memorial letter opener his mother had gotten him from one of those god-awful *But wait!* television ads.

"Oh, my, are you all right, Silas?" she asked with exceptional phony tenderness. He'd already invented *pretend-erness* to characterize the mayor. That produced a smile. He didn't *look* words up; he *made* them up. The sign of a man at the top.

"One: I'm fine," he warbled through gritted teeth. "And two: I am currently teaching Mister Kimbel to fly journalistically. Flying with such grace as you would require might take some time. But I'll be sure to coach him on the finer aspects of political inuendo, nuance, and abiding need."

"Oh, you are so wonderful, Silas. I knew you would come through for me. We will have to get together for a nice round of golf at the club, you and me. And I do so like well-rounded men like yourself. Talk to you again soon. Bye."

The Mercies had come just in the nick of time. Silas considered golf the most ridiculous pursuit of absolutely nothing to exist on Planet Earth. He hated it—hated it—hated it. On top of that, *well-rounded*, indeed. A little aging and a lot of gravity. He really did not like that woman.

So what could happen next, he wondered as he applied more Kleenex to his wound. He needed to vent and, on cue, in walked Mister Stones.

Silas was so steamed about Mayor Sallie, and Kimbel was the nearest human being. Treadwell felt perfectly warranted to jump full into his shit.

"What in the flying fuck do you want?"

Kimbel stopped and in a perfectly calm voice said, "Wet dream go dry on you?"

Treadwell wondered if his Hirohito knife was balanced for throwing. He was prepared to find out. But the humor in the whole thing cracked his time-weathered countenance into a semblance of a smile, and then he laughed.

And he laughed. And he laughed.

"Alright." He waved at the new hire. "Come on in. Sit yourself down. What's up is that I can't wait until I figure out a way to waste that mother of all mayors down at City Hall."

"I was talking with Tram. He says the economic crap that is hitting San Diego, L.A., Sacramento, and D.C. is starting to show its ugly face around San Ernestino. He's starting to see *For Lease* signs on Main Street, and he says that just doesn't happen in California's best tourist town. Some of the parents that commute north or south to the cities are getting pink slips. The pickings are getting so slim in those other places, gangs are starting in on *our* town."

"We don't have a way to put this all together and do a little shaming of the venerable mayor? She still goes on like ours is a Disney property called *Perfectland* where angels come to die."

"I have an idea."

"Crap," Treadwell thought out loud. "Advertising is down 18% from last year, and it's not looking any better for the holiday season. The only people that have any money are the crooks. Pretty soon, the good folks will need to start robbing *them*. It's not a good time for me to afford new ideas, son."

"It's no big deal." He started for the door.

"Alright. Sit yourself back down."

"You're sure?"

"Stones. Give."

"I'm just fleshing it out, anyway. Right now, it looks like it will be one of those good news, better news ideas. The *good* kind that increases circulation *and* advertising. And the *better* translates into no increase in costs to the owner." He smiled, turned, and left, closing the door behind him.

"Wait! Wait!" Treadwell yelled. The guy had thrown out the bait, set the hook, and then left him hanging. Only bastards do that. But, the editor reasoned, Kimbel Stones was a good bastard.

CHAPTER 24

Finally another day in America's finest village. Sallie rocked back in her $2,500 black leather chair, clasped her hands behind her head, and, with closed eyes, thought toward the future. She could envision the designer clothes from Rodeo Drive coupled with the stretch limos and the adoring crowd. Politics would assure her ride to celebrity status.

"Hey, Willie. Come in here. Close the door," she called out.

"Yes, ma'am," Willie came back as he sauntered over to Sallie's desk. "What's up?"

"Willie, sit down. Please."

Willie thought, Oh, crap. She's giving me the final finger.

But, instead of the final finger, Sallie reached into a lower drawer and pulled out a bottle.

"This is a step up for you, gay guy. This is what comes after getting the job done accompanied with major, successful sucking up. The third rung on the ladder of political success is ... ta-da ... sharing a drink with the boss."

She withdrew a couple of Crystal D'Arques old-fashioned glasses and proceeded to pour three fingers of Balmenach 12-year-old Scotch whisky.

"That's classy stuff, your Mayor-ship."

He held the glass up to the light to observe the golden hue.

"You will find this to be of medium to heavy body, with a taste of chestnut and honey. Note how the light highlights the amber liquid with reddish hues. Also, note that I brought this back personally from the little town of Cromdale on the upper River Spey. It was a souvenir on a much needed cultural exchange trip to Scotland. We were, of course, looking for a sister city in that region with which to share whatever. I didn't pay a penny of our good city's treasured fortunes; the distillery was more than happy to take care of my needs. You will be me someday, Willie, so pay attention to the finer points."

Willie did not quite know how to read the mayor at this moment, but, when in doubt, go with the flow. "It is excellent," he feigned intimate knowledge. "I must continue to work hard and suck up."

After six fingers had passed her lips, Sallie started to relax and her conversation topic shifted to the personal. "Willie, I don't personally give a crap who you screw or suck or whatever you do, but remember this—always focus on the politics of it all. Pull in all you can and cover your sorry ass at all times. I learned the hard way. My dad was a drinker, but not the good stuff. He really didn't care what it was. He took it out on mom and, bless her heart, she stuck with him through it all."

Willie was doing his best to pretend to care. He was losing focus, trying to keep up with the mayor as she kept refilling her glass *and* his. But he listened.

"It was my father. I had to get out. I couldn't take it anymore, and I guess that whole experience at home, plus getting out on my own early, gave me the chops to get where I am. I used to call mom, trying to catch her when he wasn't home. She'd try not to cry. She'd ask me how I was and all. It was taking a real heavy toll on her."

Willie wondered if the tough as nails mayor would break down and cry. It seemed that was where they were headed. But she did not. She was too strong for that. She just continued on, her words taking on a slight slur.

"She told me in one of the last conversations I had with her that the police had taken him to jail. Domestic abuse had become a crime, and a neighbor turned him in. I guess they heard and saw too much. He was tried and convicted, and I never saw him again. Her neither. She died a week after he went to prison."

Lieutenant Willie now felt drowsy. He had filed away everything she had said, but he needed out of there and into some serious sack time.

Sallie picked up on the lack of attentiveness across her desk and told Willie he could take off. "See you mun-ya-na, soldier," she said.

As he stumbled out the door, he heard her mumble something like, "I needed the bastard. I needed my father."

CHAPTER 25

Later that night—after the mayor finished her repartee with Willie—the angry owner of one of San Ernestino's few palatial estates smashed a high-end crystal glass against his fireplace, then pounded the keys of his Smartphone. The recipient of the call was always available.

"This is McCracken," said the dark voice on the cell phone. And the tone was not pleasant.

"I don't know which part of 'sell me your property now or else' they don't get. And I don't care. This time, make sure the whole place goes. Watch 'em. Make it another black ops trick, but I want that damn fifty-year-old trailer wannabe burned to the ground. I want them to know it's arson. I want them to throw in the friggin' towel. Do you understand?"

His voice turned appreciably louder as he ramped up. John McCracken was used to getting his way. He was beyond pissed at people he considered stubborn immigrants.

The recipient man in black knew what he needed to do. He ignored the emotional claptrap. The boss man could rant all he wanted. The hired man just wanted to do the job, and have the earned funds split between his account at the Bank of Tahiti, and his other *banque polynésienne*, Socredo. He smiled at his linguistic mastery, which he'd gained as a soldier of fortune adjunct to the French Foreign Legion.

He switched his focus back to the work at hand.

Since McCracken thought black ops had to do with lights-out, night work, Beener Jackman would work it just like last time. Except, this time he would put on surveillance until the Hans left the property. Thus far, no need to terminate them.

And so it went. He waited until dark and then drove over in his black ops attire. He parked close enough to surveille the Hans' home, but would not put on his ski mask until later when he'd exited the truck. Anyone who drove by might find a man sitting in a truck and wearing a ski mask a bit suspicious, and report him. He had taken note of the Neighborhood Watch signs.

After only one hour, his patience paid off. He saw movement. The Han car pulled back from the garage and, as the Misses got in, he saw them both clearly in the dome light.

Damn! They'd left on the living room light, which spilled out into the yard. Ingress and egress would be a bigger challenge than he liked.

Still, his boss didn't want to hear about challenges. He wanted to hear about success. His first-time success versus the Hans was good history. This was now, and the point scoring system had reset to zero.

As he approached the house, he pulled out his mask. Before he could put it on, he heard a dog yap. Under the lonely street lamp half a block away came what he characterized as some stupid woman with her drop-kickable yap dog. Shit! She probably had a gun. More women carried them now, being liberated and all.

His options were down to just one. Down he went. Tying his shoe. Looking down prevented any view of his face.

He expected her to scream, and the rabid little bastard of a dog would attack. He would have no trouble ringing its scrawny little neck, right along with hers. Still, it would be hard to explain the contents of his back pack if officers arrived before he could get away.

Even a father confessor wouldn't buy his I-use-this-incendiary-stuff-for-campfires story.

But she just walked on by, said "Hi" and he could see that her white knuckled hand held one of those mace sprayers they gave away on television. He kept his head down, mumbling a response. He didn't want her to recognize his voice at a later time. Like in a lineup.

He had resisted leaping at the dog and tearing off its little appendages. On the Han property again, he looked around and saw no one. Even the yapper had disappeared into the distance. This time he placed his charges carefully around the entire house. That included climbing over a six-foot high fence twice, which, he considered, should be worth a bonus.

As he started to drive away to find a safe observation site, he caught lights in his rear view mirror. He ducked down in the seat in case it was a night patrol or that damn reporter tenant.

McCracken hadn't forbidden killing him. Jackman felt that these little town newspapers were nothing but a nuisance and had felt like burning a note in the Han's front lawn in the shape of *the finger* followed by ***Report this!***

Since overt emotional expressions did not work well with his chosen profession, he let it pass.

When the lights failed to light up his cab as the car passed, he sat up.

"*Crap!*" he spat.

The car turned back into the Hans driveway. Han's wife exited, waving her arms as if she'd forgotten something. She unlocked the door and entered. Then bang, bang, bang, bang went the incendiary devices. Misses Han was already inside when they exploded. She yelled, grabbing her side. She was hit.

"*Crap! Crap!*"

Her husband jumped out of the car and rushed after her. The anguish in the man was audible even down the street.

The black pickup took off even as the house started to light up with flames in every room.

"*Crap! Crap! Crap!*"

CHAPTER 26

Across town, the City Council meeting resembled all of the others before it. The number of townspeople attending exhibited an upward trend due to the external economic woes finally assaulting the tourist, surfing, and retirement haven known as San Ernestino. All of the council members, and the mayor, and the deputy mayor were present.

A short, fat councilman ranted on about things beyond the council's control biting it in the backside. They were losing jobs and losing tourists at an alarming rate. He was getting call after call from citizens airing their complaints. The surfers did not call. They, as usual, were doing just fine. They could still count to eleven and, sure enough, every eleventh wave was a rider.

Stones started to take interest when the topic changed to a particular land use and rezoning issue with regard to McCracken Construction. It seemed a project that had been rammed through the City Council for high-density condos on the bluff had hit a snag. McCracken had not been able to secure all of the requisite property, and the permits would expire in just twenty days.

Stones felt a tingle. At first, he thought he was getting aroused looking at the mayor. But then he realized the vibration emanated from his pants pocket.

He'd set his cell phone on vibrate, given the reverence accorded to the City Council venue, and it pulsed incessantly. He extracted it. A text message with an URGENT tag glared up at him.

The message nearly stopped his heart. It was from Tram, who monitored police and fire dispatches even after work. Given the hour, Tram had shown himself to be dedicated, to say the least.

The message read: "Fire Han res. Bad. Hans at hospital. Both in ER. On my way to Town Hall to take your place."

Stones couldn't wait for Tram. He grabbed his gear and rushed from the building. Tram had not specified the hospital. There was only one.

Weather-wise, San Ernestino's sole meteorologist produced the chronic report daily: "Seventy-Two Degrees Fahrenheit, Partly Cloudy, Or Sunny." She could have replaced it with, "Tomorrow Will Be Exactly Like Today."

And so it had been that morning.

Unknown to the weather service, a major storm had swung around from the northwest and set its sights on San Ernestino.

The rain began to pour as Stones pulled his jacket over his head, and sprinted for his car.

He fish-tailed from the slick parking lot surface onto Main Street—the only pathway to the hospital.

"This can't get any worse," he said.

Traffic lights that had been working perfectly switched off.

Then, they flashed.

Drivers who'd skipped the page on flashing traffic lights in their DMV booklets fabricated a maze for Stones to dart through.

His heart wanted to explode.

He cursed himself for creating the bad karma with his previous statement.

Stones recalled the pounding heart syndrome from his experience on the Bering Sea islands.

To remain intact, and in control. That had got him through.

"Come on, Quentin! Come on, Bettie! Hang tight! I'm coming as fast as I can!"

He swerved to miss a side-sliding fire truck.

Almost ready to give up, he remembered his Diomede mantra.

"It's never this cold!"

CHAPTER 27

Parking at the hospital posed no problem. In his current mental state, thinking did.

Stones ran through the torrent of rain to the emergency entrance. There, he extracted directions to the first floor emergency area from an ambulance driver returning to his vehicle.

Aware of the Han backstory, he hoped it would provide him the means to get by the gatekeepers.

The man in an obvious hurry rushed to the nurses' station and interrupted a red-headed RN.

"Miss! Miss!"

A startled woman in white moved to block his way.

"I was informed that Mister and Misses Han were brought here. I'm here visiting. I'm their son." He caught his breath. Enough to take the exclamation out of his voice. "Please tell me what room they are in."

The nurse checked him out, but did not seem too concerned. Dealing with people and their problems was the unfortunate normal in her line of work. And it had already been a long day.

"First of all, I'm not 'Miss', I'm Cooper," she informed him, pointing to the Velcro label on her tunic. "And since I recorded them in, and since they are both decidedly Asian, and since you are not... unless you have one hell of a trick explanation, it's not going to happen," she admonished in her best RN-cum-drill instructor tone.

Stones knew he could cause some serious damage, but he kept his cool. He also knew he came armed with the requisite resourceful nature of a spy.

"My parents died. The Hans are my foster parents. And, if you need more than that, I can wake my boss, the editor of the *Observer*, and..."

Cooper saw the ID he continued to flash, bought the story, and led him down the hall.

"Sit here." She gestured to a bank of six interconnected you-don't-want-to-sit-here-very-long chairs.

A reluctant Stones complied.

She entered through double doors under the sign, EMERGENCY ROOM.

When she returned, so did a man dressed in doctor green. Fresh blood splotched his tunic, but Kimbel assumed it was probably chicken's blood put there to impress nurses and loved ones of the stricken.

"Hi. I'm Doctor Patel," said a shortish, dark-skinned man of Indian descent. "Mister Han obtained some burns to his legs while attempting to rescue his wife, I'm afraid."

"What do you mean—burns, rescue?" Kimbel found himself gasping for breath. "What... what happened?"

"Here's what I have at this point. Fire Marshal Booker reported his initial findings as some manner of explosions at the Han's home. A flash fire started, and Mister Han rescued his wife from being burned to death. He sustained burns to his legs, but no secondary trauma. Misses Han suffered some second-degree burns. In addition, she was struck by flying debris, which fractured her pelvis. They are in recovery now, but under sedation. They can not see anyone."

"Are they…" The words drifted off as Kimbel feared the worst.

"Their situation is stable, both of them. Their prognosis is that both will survive. At this point, we don't know if either of them will suffer permanently," the doctor said.

"Nothing else? That's all? That's it?"

"I'm sorry." Doctor Patel turned away. Just before he re-entered the ER, he paused and looked down at the floor.

"Mister Han did try to say something. I mean, he asked about his wife. Then, he said something like 'crack in' like he was trying to talk about a crack in something that might have caused the fire. Those were his last words before we sedated him."

"Anything else, Doctor?"

"One thing. It's strange, though. The fire marshal said Mr. Han was outside the residence, but Mrs. Han was inside when this all happened. He couldn't say for sure it was an accident."

Stones shook his head at the possibility.

"I must get back now. We're busy tonight." The doctor turned and disappeared through the large ER doors.

Kimbel Stones stumbled back to the chairs, trying to make any sense out of the doctor's comments. But he could not think. He hung his head. Wait! Another fire. Low probability. And the words: *crack in*.

His analytical mind shoved aside the emotional component that had taken charge.

Could it be?

Could it be that, under the dire circumstances, Mister Han had attempted to mouth the word McCracken? The developer? The same man trying for a permit extension at tonight's City Council meeting. The same man that had been leaning hard on the Hans for their property.

By God, that was it!

Mc*Cracken*!

"Ok, buddy," Stones seethed through his teeth. "Game on!"

He smacked his fist into his palm, jumped up, and headed for the door.

"For you and all of those unlucky enough to be hooked up with you. *Game fucking on!*" he snarled.

CHAPTER 28

Stones drove out of the hospital with mixed emotions. He felt sorry for the wonderful couple who'd unselfishly raised him in his parents' absence. He was no longer the man they'd known all those years. With the Diomede operation, he'd departed the mindset of the mild-mannered individual in the NSA's Fort Meade, Maryland, Black Cube, who'd ridden a desk and delivered dispassionate analytic reviews, for one that embraced violence and adrenaline. He'd allowed himself to become enraged with whomever had visited their crap on his dear friends. His objectivity became an unwitting victim.

He knew he would have to let the sorrow erode on its own. The anger, however, he felt compelled to stoke. First, there was a place he needed to go. He drove from the hospital west to the Coast Highway. He turned left, continuing down the vacant expanse of land until he reached the Han's home. Even in the darkness of a moonless night, it looked pitiful.

He could not survey the damage up close. Police yellow tape surrounded the site. From the street, though, he could easily tell that the home had been completely destroyed. The stench of wet burnt wood filled the air to the point that Kimbel left. His heart sounded its war drum now. He needed to clear his head enough to conjure up an appropriate battle plan.

He made a U-turn and headed back north. Along the way, he stopped at a 7/11 to pick up some supplies and some liquor. Then, he checked into the local motel—one where no one he knew would look for him—just up the highway. The Crazy 8 was neither fancy nor a dump. His room was clean and functional, a lot like San Ernestino.

With just a pad of paper, a pen, and a bottle of Bacardi, he began to plan. He remembered an old rhyme from his college days: "The time has come to drink some rum." He poured the Bacardi 151 straight—no cubes, no mix. It was the sailor's old standby. He needed to calm down sufficiently in order to construct some serious tactical plans.

Stones' first notion was to conjure up some righteous violence. He knew that none of the San Ernestino perps could match the kind of governmental mayhem that passed for a standard field op. The Hans had taught him that, when subtle is possible, it is preferred to direct pain.

In fact, Kimbel, in true American fashion, had interpreted that to mean that more righteous pain could be delivered by means other than physical violence. With them in mind, he set about laying the wood on these perpetrators in a severe but non-physical way.

• • •

In the end, he knew he would need three chunks of intel. First, he would require a list of the participants involved in the plan to initially intimidate the Hans, and then to burn them out, perhaps even kill them. He already knew the developer named McCracken had failed to secure the property from them for a major and lucrative development plan. The man had pushed very hard, sending emissaries to the Hans' home. He'd witnessed the attempt by a man calling himself Mark Smithson. They'd received a series of pressuring phone calls, but they stood firm. Kimbel knew from living room chats with the Hans about these attempts.

Second, he needed to identify them all. No innocent parties would be hurt. And he also intended to learn what every one of them stood to gain. The paper would provide him the resources he needed to get backstories on everyone.

Lastly, he needed to discover their weaknesses. The points of pain unique to each individual. That included where they were vulnerable and what would make them hurt. Really hurt.

CHAPTER 29

It would be a very busy day. Valentina Kummonova knew that. Having already purchased a large suitcase, stylish dresses and shoes, black slacks and pastel tops at the Sovietskaya Shopping District, she'd checked in at Korsakov's premier Hotel Alfa. The proprietor spoke very good English, which gave her a chance to practice. She would need this.

She'd run over to the bank to exchange some rubles for American dollars. Virtual reconnaissance informed her that the ship terminal provided no exchange or ATM kiosks. She needed dollars.

Back at the hotel, it took her little time to fill the suitcase, apply a lock, and push it into the closet. A short walk, and she was ready to calm her racing pulse at the well-attended Penguin Bar on nearby October Street. She asked for an American drink.

The bartender placed a three-quarter-filled pint beer glass and a filled shot glass on the bar in front of her.

"It's called a Depth Charge," he had informed her. "You take the whiskey shot glass, and you carefully drop it into the beer. Then, you drink."

Two of those did the trick. As she struggled to walk back to her hotel, she wondered if the American she sought might be a little stronger than the text books indicated.

The new day dawned on Valentina toting her baggage along Soviet Street—apparently, the news of the USSR collapse in 1989 hadn't reached this far—and past Lenin Square. A jog to the left and then right onto Reidovy Lane, she stopped to wonder if her efforts would be worthwhile.

The young woman who arrived at the Morvokzal cruise ship terminal didn't possess the Slavic appearance of the European Russians. With good reason. She'd been born on this, the east Siberian island of Sakhalin, not far from this port. Quite bright, she'd received a scholarship to the University of Moscow. There, she met Vladimir, future president of the Russian Federation.

They met, they connected, and didn't disconnect until three days later. But that was then.

Now, standing ashore of the Silversea cruise liner, Silver Shadow, she produced her perfectly created documentation as a translator duly dispatched by the Korsakovsky District of Sakhalin Oblast. It indicated she was to accompany a diplomat heading on a Trans-Pacific cruise to Anchorage, Alaska. The diplomat, Igor Mikhailovich Grubkin, could not fly due to a chronic ailment, and his usual Russian-English interpreter had taken ill just that morning.

Valentina's documents indicated her to be Tatiana Sergeyevna Popich, just in case the situation at the SVR lab caused her real name to be on someone's watch list. There would be no problem remembering the cover name and its nickname, Tanya. She'd used it to play S & M games with Vladi.

Clearly, she would travel a long distance in her quest to find the American, Kimbel Stones. She'd work that from Anchorage. When she arrived just eight days hence.

As she walked up the gangway, she caught sight of the Eins Soya ferry, headed for Hokkaido, Japan. It was a trip she had promised herself someday. Perhaps after Mr. Stones. If she lived.

"*Dobriy vyecher*, Comrade," she said when she'd been shown to Igor's stateroom on the top deck. She noted that they were alone, and that he was not the fat, stubby individual she'd expected. Instead, he was tall and lean. And muscular. He didn't look at all like the stereotypical desk jockeys of the Federation's state department. Not at all.

"And good evening to you, Tanya. May I call you by your short name?"

His response stopped her cold. "Your English is perfect." She turned her head a bit to one side. "I am interpreter."

"And a good one, I understand."

"You are not diplomat?"

"In brief, no. But you don't… can't know any more than that. You shall interpret what I say, when it becomes necessary, and I shall pretend not to understand a word of the English. Now, please. Get undressed. Our ship shall disembark shortly. You and I shall attend the Sail-Away party topside. First, we try out the teak balcony. Then, the party. Right after we shower."

Valentina was dumbstruck. What had she gotten herself into?

Her crazy idea to go after the American had just turned sharp left. Or right. She wasn't sure which.

She said something to herself in Russian that quickly translated itself into, Oh, my God.

Then, the realization hit.

Govno!… Shit!

• • •

Valya's exit had been easy. With the ship having made its way into Anchorage in the early hours, she joined the early-off passengers with Igor still contentedly asleep in their top-deck suite. She planned to use her diplomatic 'go anywhere' U.S. visa to purchase an airline ticket south.

She hopped a cab to the Ted Stevens Anchorage International Airport—just five miles southwest of town—and found her place at the end of a long, serpentine security line. It seemed another cruise ship had snookered hers, debarking a half-hour earlier.

Due to the overwhelming din of the terminal's denizens, a wall-mounted big screen displayed the English language, close-captioned rendition of whatever was being said.

Valya was not an operative and had never received any such training. Still, to get herself back in with Vladimir, she needed to create this covert operation. Once done, and with him aware, he'd take her back to Moscow. She'd give him new children.

As if on cue, a blink of the big screen, and there he was. The big smile. And a slender and quite beautiful woman standing beside him. Smiling, also.

Valya's heart fluttered.

It got worse.

The text below: "Vladimir's New Sweetheart."

Her head went light. She steadied herself, grasped the arm of a large man next to her, then coughed an apology in her native language. She peered into his blank stare.

"I must succeed," she said. "I shall have new skills."

The screen had centered the Russian president's new flame.

Valya glared.

"I will use them—those skills—in Moscow. On her."

• • •

Picking either the Los Angeles airport or the San Diego rendition 120 miles south had been decided for her. Of the two, the San Diego flight was first out, but in just twenty minutes. She hustled, and just barely made the plane.

The first class seat, courtesy of the Russian Federation, would've had her shot in the days of the Communists. All were to be treated exactly the same except, of course, the power elite.

During the flight, Valya listened intently to the other passengers, the in-flight announcements, and the small television screen facing her. She picked up the English in every case, and felt ready for the more challenging aspects of the tasks ahead.

She never feared flying. However, the approach to the San Diego airport flew by office buildings so close and so low, she waved at the occupants. The landing, as the airliner barely passed above a few four-story parking garages, turned out to be unremarkable. She knew only the best pilots were allowed to attempt this heart-thumping venue.

After wandering about in San Diego's modern, artistically designed facility, she asked directions from someone she was sure would not place her east Russian accent, rented a car with GPS, and drove the surface streets north. She steered clear of the ominous and infamous Southern California freeway system.

She would have him. Kimbel Stones. Soon.

CHAPTER 30

For the time being, at least, Stones had a moment to himself. Whether that was good or not, he didn't know. He shifted his cut-crystal glass, half full of rum, and closed his eyes.

Even with the light shut out, his mind produced a vision of presents under a Christmas tree. His wife's, from the day of her death several years before, still unopened. Her's were the only ones.

Funny how the grief he felt now for the Hans surfaced other grief from the past. Stones stared at the electric fireplace across the hotel room. He thought back.

Christmas Eve. His parents arriving outside. His new bride, Molly, rushing out to meet them. A fresh snow topped an invisible ¼" glaze of ice.

He imagined the freaked look on his dad's face as he hit the brakes.

The old Buick Roadmaster lost adhesion. The car slid out of control.

No sounds. A loud crunch.

Inside his home, Stones heard nothing. The pounding on the door had him outside in seconds.

There stood his mother with a look of horror he'd never seen before.

Beyond, his father, a deeply religious carpenter, knelt next to the battered body.

"It just slid, Son. It just slid."

Stones had summoned 911. The ambulance arrived in minutes. After assuring no spinal injury, they strapped her to a gurney and thrust her into the vehicle.

Before Stones could jump in with her, it happened.

The flashing EMS lights clicked off.

Just like that.

Gone.

There'd been no merriment that night. Just sitting. Staring.

He changed. Investing in someone, then feeling that magnitude of hurt, disappeared from his radar. The event propelled him into the world of secrets. If the spy agencies wanted him in harm's way in some foreign hell-hole, fine. There'd be no one to await the phone call or the direct message. "With deepest regrets. The love of your life is dead—US Form 92675."

When Stones placed his graduate education and intellect on the dotted line, he anticipated that the CIA might want him. Or the DIA. He figured his analytic skills would impress more so than his physical attributes. The NSA summoned him. No foreign hell-holes, they'd promised. Just the good old East Coast.

His father had taught him to take his problems inside, especially the toughest ones, and not to share them with anyone. "Chew 'em up and spit 'em out," he'd said.

It was difficult not to follow that advice, but this was the Hans. This was blood.

He called Susanna.

• • •

She arrived twenty minutes later, entering the partially open door as he refilled his glass.

"Rum?"

"No, thanks. Let's talk."

It amazed him that on short notice, she still appeared in cover girl perfection.

She cocked her head slightly to the right. Inquisitive.

"You've got the look," he said.

"What look?" She took a second. "It's been a while, hasn't it?"

"Maybe this isn't a good idea." He stood, hoisted his coat over his shoulder, and turned toward the door.

"I'm here, too. Where you are. You lost someone."

He stopped. Listened.

"It was a while ago, wasn't it? Still, you can't let go of her."

Clearly, the blonde woman who always appeared ready and able for a glamour magazine cover shoot possessed intellect atop her striking good looks.

"I'm sorry. I didn't mean to drag baggage into this. It's not right."

"*Au contraire*. I'm a listener. Here." She patted the bed. "Sit."

He did.

"Talk."

He related the story of the Christmas Tree and the presents. Of his father and mom trying out their new GPS to the digs of their son, and the wife they'd never met. And the rest.

Susanna extracted the glass from his hand.

He dropped his head into his hands.

She downed the rum.

"There's more, isn't there? Something triggered your feelings."

He told her about the Hans. Nearly killed. Nearly torn from his life.

She felt a surge of empathy for him in the moments before. She'd had someone in her heart once. It hit close to home. Much too close.

CHAPTER 31

Kimbel Stones and Susanna Thomson sat in silence for what seemed to them no more than thirty seconds, when Stones' phone rang.

His heart jumped.

Susanna plucked the device from his coat pocket and touched the answer icon. She handed it to him with a nod that said, "Go ahead."

"Who is this?" asked an anxious Kimbel Stones.

"Bonus Jack."

Stones recognized the handshake phrasing from Magic Man's CIA boss. An operation a few years before.

He examined his iSTU satellite phone for answers. Nothing to help. He responded.

"You've got the wrong number."

"It's snowing in San Diego," said the voice.

"It's that time of year."

"Nice to know you. Your old unit contacted me as liaison on the Russian caper. *Ostrová Gvozdyeva*?"

"Big Diomede."

"Yeah. The larger of the two islands."

"I'm on extended leave, Bonus Jack. Call back in a year."

"This can't wait. SVR traffic indicates some small nuclear weapons are in development. We don't know where just yet. Kimbel, that Vladimir fellow really wants Alaska back."

Stones knew well the Russian foreign intelligence service. The NSA had deployed huge new computing capabilities just to decrypt SVR signals intercepts. So, they were operational.

"Who were the endpoints of the comms?"

"Moscow. With that Big Diomede output as content to Pyongyang."

"North Korea." Stones knew well what a wild card that country represented. "What do you have, Jack?"

"Seems the Russians are upset. The miniature nukes they've uncovered aren't theirs, and the Koreans don't have the technology."

"There's more, isn't there?"

"My boss said you were sharp."

"Cut to the chase."

"It's a communist deal. That leaves Laos, Vietnam, Cuba, and…"

"China."

"Give the man an egg roll. It appears the Chinese have developed what I've labeled mini-nukes no bigger than a football, or a rugby ball if you're a Brit. Five megatons is the estimate."

"Like I said, I'm busy. But I know who to contact at NSA to start the ball rolling for you. I'll touch base, and get back to you in a week. Ciao bella, Jack."

Click.

"Pretend you didn't hear that."

Absent an acknowledgment, Stones turned to see Susanna seated in a chair, purse pistol pointed at the ceiling, her elbow cradled in the other hand.

Keeping their eyes locked, she slowly turned her head and blew across the barrel. "Mossad. At 18. Youngest ever. Retired two years later. Moved here."

He collected his breath.

A lot to process in a couple of minutes.

Jack, and now this.

He knew from his days as liaison between the NSA and the CIA that it was most often best to act unconcerned, unafraid, and calm when the other party wielded the gun.

"You are by far the most elegant and visibly beautiful young woman I've ever come to know. Honestly, I sensed a backstory. But Mossad?"

"Kidon."

"Jesus! An assassin turned advertising specialist."

"So, I can walk and chew gum."

"Why didn't I guess?"

"We can do backstories another time. For now, it goes down like this. You showed me yours and I showed you mine. Even Steven. Okay?"

"*Ack* on that one." He shook his head. "*Ack* means—"

"*Ack* means positive acknowledgment. *Nak* is negative. I know."

"How's about we get back to being our newspaper selves and tone it down a notch?"

She returned the weapon to her purse, and started with her buttons. "How's about we get physical?"

• • •

Three thousand miles east at Fort Meade, Maryland, an NSA operative with the unlikely title of Legacy Mainframe Wizard, retained her Chinese-heritage reserve and tapped her tablet computer twice. Her signal—vectored through her civilian friend at Lipschitz Private Investigations—dropped. The image feed from the Stones and Susanna TV popped black. She'd get the call from Mr. Kimbel Stones regarding the Russians alright, but it paid to stay ahead of the game. And knowing her adversary for Stones' affections provided an advantage. Someday, she'd be Mrs. Stones. She felt quite sure of that.

CHAPTER 32

A new day had dawned, and the mayor was pissed. She'd received word about the fire at the Hans' place that nearly killed them both. With an election coming up, and her planned coup, she could not have this developer thing getting out of hand. She gave instruction to her minion Willie to call McCracken and get him in *Now!*

He had arrived twenty minutes prior, but she chose to let him sit in the anteroom. She had gone over in her mind what she wanted to let fly and the time had come. She buzzed her boy Friday and told him to show the developer in.

"How're things, Misses Mayor?" he pretended to want to know.

"You stupid fuck!" was all the diplomacy she could muster. "***Arson Begets Murder*** is the headline that nearly came to pass. Your soon-to-be-a-eunuch tough guy nearly screwed the pooch last night. And it is my experience that nearly screwed pooches can grow into pit bulls. And then they bite."

"Whoa," he said, stepping back. "I think we're getting off on the wrong vibe here."

Before he could add to his defensive posture, she wailed in at him again. "There is no wrong foot when it's sticking up your ass, John. My plans are to win the next election, which, as you may or may not realize, requires a change in the city Charter. Around here, we elect three council members. One of us serves as Mayor for a two year term, rotating the job until all have served. Then, we conduct another election."

Her chest heaved and a bright red coloration illuminated her professionally applied war paint.

"I, clever woman that I am, have figured out how to accomplish that, and I won't have some pick and shovel guy screwing it up. Do you understand me?"

McCracken had seen tirades before, but he admitted to himself that this one approached 10 on the Olympic scale. He needed to either calm her down or let her have a few days to get her shit back together. He knew she liked a little pot now and then, and that a younger man supplied at McCracken Development expense would have her eating out of his hand once again. He'd done it before, and this time would be no different.

"Sallie, I'm truly sorry. It got out of hand. The son-of-a-bitch that screwed us both with his incompetence is paid off and long gone," he lied. "He is not a problem. Now, c'mon. I know what you want, and I will be there for you. All the money you need for your next conquest. Mayor, governor, whatever you want."

Sallie was starting to get her breathing back to normal, especially when she heard the word *governor*. She glanced around at the paintings that adorned her office walls, all with a Western flair. Even the Remington bronze on her desk typified her pioneer spirit and outlaw heart.

"Look, you need a little weekender to get it back. On me. Just like before. Catalina Island is beautiful this time of year. Twenty-six miles. Right off the coast. You can use my plane," he finished, sounding like a brother offering solace to a sister. Or a father to a daughter.

The mayor paced the room, as if trying to expend the adrenaline that still coursed through her veins. Finally, she stopped. She understood.

"You're right, John," she said, composure regained. "I'll put out the fires—no pun intended—by Friday. Then, I'm out of here." She threw an uncharacteristically natural little smile at him. "You know me. I'll be back Monday, ready to swing for the fence again."

"I'll arrange for a flight out of Palomar Airport Friday night. As you know, my pilot is a former Top Gun graduate—one of the best. He'll take care of everything, including those special perks you love." He withdrew a round tin from his jacket pocket. "This designer version of pot enhances the experience…" He winked. "…if you know what I mean."

They parted company. Outside the mayor's office, McCracken smiled at the young man who was covering Willie Sample for a bathroom break. It was just a quick glance. He failed to notice that the intern did not return the smile. Once McCracken was gone, the young man flipped off the intercom button.

Sometimes life, like politics, just sucked.

• • •

Sallie made it to the airport on Friday evening. In short order, she climbed aboard the plane and was winging her way to Catalina. She knew from experience that McCracken would have set her up in a gorgeous suite on a hill with a look-down view of Avalon Bay. Suitable companionship awaited her, ready to take her to heaven.

The flight proved relaxing with the help of a few stiff drinks. Before re-entering the flight deck, the attendant couldn't help but observe. "Same brand your father drank."

Sallie hurled the glass, striking a window. Dead silence. She dropped her head in her hands, and wept.

• • •

The jet cruised in to Catalina Island at landing speed as if it would strike the steep cliff below the runway. But the excellent pilot rotated the plane back slightly and touched it down without the slightest hint of a bump.

The mayor excitedly deplaned and entered the transportation vehicle. Being mayor definitely had its perks.

CHAPTER 33

While the confrontation was hitting the fan at City Hall, Kimbel dragged himself into the paper—dense fog hangover and all. His plan required serious research and he headed for the editor's office for guidance. He did not, however, share his plans. The editor would have headed him off. Still, Silas Treadwell could not fire him given what had just happened to his substitute family.

"I need to do some background research," Kimbel began.

He had a look that Treadwell read as engaged. Good.

"I need to do the ground work that all good reporters do when they are covering significant people. I've extracted some things from the Internet," he continued, "but it is mostly fluff and too recent. Where do I pull intelligence going back a couple of decades?"

At once impressed and concerned, Treadwell did not expect such dedication to duty. "You need to check the morgue. Goes back to the mid-90's. Tram knows it well, but he is out on assignment. See if Luisa has some time."

"Thanks. You won't regret it," he said.

Treadwell registered a red flag, but it might just as well have been waving frantically under water. The older man's mind shifted forward. He waved Kimble away.

Kimbel departed the editor's office and moved with purpose into Luisa's domicile. She would make time, she said, and off they went, Luisa in the lead.

The morgue at any newspaper is where old stories go to die. Out of respect for the stories, they reside there throughout eternity or until the paper crumbles. The *Observer* crew made microfiche from the paper copies until about four years prior, at which point they scanned them into a computer. The computer was then used to archive the stories onto single-write DVD discs.

The room, off to the side of the building, contained three tables arranged one at a time. The first table held three microfiche viewers. The second, three desktop computers, and the third accommodated laying out the few print newspapers that remained. In modern times, the paper provided Internet access to the computerized stories and typically received several hits a week—on the whole system.

"I need backstory on Sallie Goddard, Mayor, and John McCracken, President of McCracken Development Company," Kimbel told Luisa.

"I proof stories about them all the time. I haven't seen anything about McCracken getting into politics. What's that all about?" she inquired.

"Yeah. There's some relationship I'm feeling between them. I think it's important, but it hasn't been reported. I need backstories to check it out."

Luisa took him by the hand and led him to the computers. "Have a seat. You can access all of our archives from here. All except for the microfiche. I'll check out the mayor for stories that mention McCracken, and you can search for McCracken stuff with Ms. Goddard."

After about 15 minutes, Kimbel sat back in his chair. "Whoa!" He stared.

Luisa leaned over to check out the screen. Her shoulder pressed against the front of his and he felt her warmth through his shirt. Her nonchalance with physical contact just added one more nail into Kimbel's coffin.

The list of story headlines on the screen indicated McCracken as a major contributor to the mayor's campaigns. As they browsed the stories, they spotted plenty of smiley-face photo opportunities that displayed their connection. But was the connection more lurid?

Luisa went back to her computer after essentially rubbing off on Kimbel. She found additional evidence of a political bond. But even the smiley-faced photos did not implicate them in some kind of a personal, make that physical, relationship. It was okay for businesses to contribute to political campaigns, but it was not okay to seek or receive payback. Kimbel knew that no one gave any meaningful amount of money to a politician without expecting something just as meaningful in return.

To discover the tit-for-tat, they would need to dig deeper. So, they moved on to the microfiche.

"How does a small town politician pay back someone like McCracken?" Kimbel posed the question. He really did not know. He'd spent his life and career in big cities.

"Either she is getting zoning changes or variances, or some other kind of change in city rules, in order to pay back McCracken. Probably a lot more than he's put in," said Luisa. "I've proofread every story that's gone to print in the last five years, and it seems to me, now that you mention it, that Mr. McCracken has pretty much gotten his way with the zoning board. But our zoning board is actually shared with the neighboring two towns. The Bookends."

"Bookends? What's that all about?"

"Yeah. The next town up and the next town down kind of frame our little burg. I call 'em the bookends. Their boundaries push up against ours and, in one way of looking at it, keep us from growing to the north or to the south. With the ocean on the west side, San E could only grow out to The Five freeway, which it's done. Everything new is redevelopment except...the land on either side of your friends."

Kimbel was beginning the get an idea of what motivated the players in San E, but the whole thing had not clicked yet. "It seems strange that McCracken can keep making money hand over fist without any growth potential," he said.

Luisa turned to face Kimbel, who sat only a foot away. Although focused, he could not help but notice that even her breath was sexy.

"Come to think of it," she continued, "he moved here from San Diego where developers get zoning changes all the time. It's somewhat of a game down there. You want to hear?" she asked with a tilt of her head.

"Yes. How these people function is a piece of the puzzle I need."

Luisa nodded. "It works like this. A developer buys a piece of land where he plans to build single family residences, he says. He promises to pay for the additional city services the development will require—a few more people, a few more cars. The city rezones the property, say from agricultural to residential. Sounds pretty good."

"Yes. That wouldn't get the public's attention at all. There's more, isn't there?"

"But he doesn't build yet. Then, a couple of years and an election or two later, he's got the people he wants on the City Council. He receives zoning changes or variances from them and, before you know it, high-density housing covers the landscape. And all of the city services he previously promised to provide become inadequate, and they get pushed back on the folks. Nice, huh? Every time these guys play, the people pay."

"So, if McCracken and Sallie are working a deal, that means." He stopped. "The election is coming up next month. I've got it!" he shouted. "That's a puzzle piece!" He leapt up from the table and ran to the door.

"What?" Luisa cried after him. But he was through the door at a dead run. "Don't you want to hear what else I found? About her being adopted? That not only were her biological parents hidden, but the adopting parents, as well?"

CHAPTER 34

Kimbel transformed from a man helping friends to a man with a mission. His heart nearly pounded out of his chest as he sat inside his motel room. When he reached a stopping point and started to review his work, he realized he needed another set of eyes, another mind to make his writing have punch. And he knew exactly who he needed. He found the number and called. She answered.

Luisa lived in an apartment about a mile from work, a simple one bedroom with a kitchen and a living room. Nothing special. But she had given it her special touch—a warm Portuguese style—which made it quite nice and cozy.

She took the call against her better judgment, surprised to discover Kimbel on the line. He sounded on the verge of bursting. As if he'd struck gold and then found a bunch of diamonds, too.

He told her he desperately needed her help. Without trying, she slipped into her natural mode of wanting to help a guy in trouble. Not that there was any trouble. No, that would come later. She invited him over.

It was nine o'clock and, clad in her nightgown, she curled up on the sofa with a good book. How she could stand reading after doing it all day was anyone's guess.

Kimbel drove to Luisa's place, ready to draw her into his grand scheme. She opened the front door and stood there, caressing the doorframe, in nothing but a filmy nightgown.

He was temporarily speechless.

She smirked with what for any other woman would have been a 'men are pigs' smirk, but felt so comfortable in her own skin, and with others, she did not even think in those terms.

"Ah. Ah," said Kimbel in what sounded like a lame impression of Odd Job from the Bond movie, Goldfinger. "Do you, ah, do you want to put something on?" he finally managed.

"Don't be silly, K. I'm perfectly fine." She twirled around for effect. She finished with her head tilted back slightly, which to Kimbel indicated her total ownership of his soul. And certain physical parts.

"Come, come." She grabbed his hand and pulled him inside, shutting the door behind them. She led him to the table.

Kimbel gratefully sat down. *Perfectly fine*, indeed, he thought.

He showed her what he'd done. In order to read his handwritten work, she moved her chair next to him. Then, she did it again. She leaned against his shoulder as she pointed at his work. Kimbel lost his focus. One more time, she questioned him about a certain sentence structure. As he turned to her, their faces were a mere three inches apart, or thereabouts.

The fires smoldering inside both of them flashed into a deep passionate kiss.

So much for work. In just a few seconds, they were sprawled on the table and acceding to the call of their passions.

Their evening proceeded from the table to the floor to the sofa to the bed.

When the clock struck twelve, they were back at the table, this time to proof his work. He departed just before two A.M. and walked into his hotel room by two-thirty. Wow. 'Never sleep with someone at work' went the mantra. Golden advice.

What struck Kimbel the most about Luisa was that every cell participated in her sexiness. She did not put on an act like other women he'd known. It was who she was. She defined sexy. How anyone could be so cool and comfortable with sexuality was beyond him.

One thing he did know. The topic required additional study.

CHAPTER 35

The next morning found Stones exiting Luisa's apartment and shortly thereafter pulling into the newspaper's parking lot. He grabbed a manila envelope he'd stopped by her place to retrieve, and was inside in less than a minute.

The editor's office was next. Without knocking—a mortal sin in Silas Treadwell's book—he flung open the door and dashed inside.

Words flew from his mouth like water from a fire hose.

"You wanna do what?" the editor exclaimed. "This is your great idea to save the paper? This is what you meant by jumpstarting our ad space and our subscriber base? Kimbel, we are not an opinion paper. No one cares about anyone's opinion in San E. The good citizens want to read some news, check out the bargains at Mrs. Humpfuck's Pet Supply Store, and then they want the remnants to be usable for making paper maché or lining bird cages."

The older man had worked up a nice red color in his cheeks, but Kimbel refused to be put off.

"It's not what you think, Chief. This town is headed down the tubes if we don't get some leadership in City Hall. City Hall is too fat, dumb, and happy to lead a Mother's Day parade. A series of opinion pieces can get them off the dime. Done properly, we can get this place turned around. Think about it. People stop losing their jobs, businesses stay in business, criminals disappear into blocks of cement and steel, and City Hall starts functioning again. That has to be good for the paper."

"First of all, you will kindly not refer to me as Chief. This isn't the Daily Fucking Planet. Second, the mayors of this town have never given a rat's ass about the people. Why should they start now?"

In the next ten seconds, Treadwell's complexion receded to pink. His calming signaled he'd glanced across his office at a wall poster from the 1960s. Alvin Lee of the hard rock group, Ten Years After, held his iconic red Gibson ES-335 guitar with a peace symbol displayed prominently. "Yes, peace," the editor muttered to himself.

"Business as usual is what they are all about," Kimbel went on. "The people of San E have already taken the first step. I've checked. You can't even get them to write Letters To The Editor. They are complacent. Sheep-like."

"That's true across the nation. So what?"

"Suppose they found out how badly they are getting screwed. It's the people that take action, not the paper. But we can light the fire." Kimbel was animated. Treadwell was not.

After the editor told Kimbel how things were going to go forward, he placed a mental check mark in the-boss-knows-all box, and considered how to introduce the first piece. Yes, he'd observed that the new reporter did have the pulse of the town. And in such a short time. Treadwell conceded, and off they went on a course that would turn out nearly impossible to steer. At least from his own perspective. Since they agreed the pieces would be most effective if they were ghost written, the editor tasked Kimbel to fabricate a by-line moniker.

The result: Dexter Freehand.

Both agreed the name posed no risk of actually existing in the English-speaking world.

Treadwell returned Stones' glance. "Dexter, it is."

Treadwell told the rest of the staff that the *Observer* would be having a new piece to address the tough socio-economic times and the inability of politics to address them. He met the common question of *who* with *mystery man*.

Treadwell created as much drama as he could. The universal response to the unusual stroke of brilliance was *Oh*.

With the team all solidly behind him, he assembled a lead-in to preface the first article.

Stones, for his part, crafted a piece that laid out, in a most succinct manner, where the good citizens of this fine country found themselves. It went like this:

> *Editor's note: Today marks the first of a series of opinion pieces, dealing with the current difficult state of affairs in a very tough economy. Severe problems exist at all levels and precious little is being done that effectively addresses the needs of the American people under these unusual and challenging circumstances.* The *Observer has acquired the exceptional talents of Mr. Dexter Freehand to put the facts in perspective for you, the citizens of San Ernestino. We encourage you to read and to respond to this series of articles. Please send your own opinions, situations, and experiences to* ***editor@thesanernestinoobserver.com****. Thank you, Silas Treadwell, Editor.*
>
> *Dear Reader. By now, every single person in the country is aware of our economic disaster. Although the economic and social crisis has struck worldwide, news coverage has kept focus on its effects at the national, state, and local levels. We have heard the countless stories relating personal disasters such as good, hardworking people losing jobs and even of several related suicides. Who caused the problem has been the second most asked question, but the number one question on everyone's mind is, "How do we stop the bleeding and get ourselves out of this?"*
>
> *The official response from Washington has been "We did not cause this, but we will address it and find our way out of this."*
>
> *Is that true? I wonder. On closer inspection, it seems the government policies associated with both personal greed and incompetence seem to be behind every problem we have. On the*

government's side, pushing for extremely loose money and holding back regulators from enforcing laws and regulations have created the problem, pure and simple.

In their relentless pursuit of the almighty vote, both political parties have conspired to buy votes and, at the same time, solicit contributions that will help them all to stay in office forever. For those not familiar, 'contribution' is the word used to describe a legal bribe. Imagine, if you will, any small amount you might send in to support a party or candidate. You get the piece asking for money and then another piece that lets you select the amount. So is it $25, is it $50, or is it some other amount? It actually does not matter. Your contribution is used to perpetuate the status quo. Every time.

Do they keep track of who you are so as to thank you personally? Of course, not. They only keep track of small donors so they can ask again. Next time. They are only motivated to track large, materially significant amounts and their donors.

Materially is an interesting word here. What it means in this context is an amount large enough that the donor expects a favor in return. Does that not sound like a bribe? It does to me. At any rate, that is the way it works in what we call the career political world—the one where the professional politicians, unlike you, put their selfish needs ahead of yours. Put another way, they put themselves before their country. Sad, but true.

I have personally seen this in Washington and at state and local levels. The problem is not the economy. It is that citizens in the early stages of this country, who went off to represent other citizens like themselves and then came home after two or four years of service, exist no more. In fact, the only contact modern politicians have with rank and file Americans comes right before every election. Elections and money are all they need us for.

Why does this matter to you? What can one person do, anyway? These are questions I regularly hear.

Look for the answers right here in upcoming revelations of how this all impacts San Ernestino and what you need to do to protect yourself and your loved ones.

Until next time, respectfully yours,
Dexter Freehand, Citizen

CHAPTER 36

Flying in John McCracken's Gulfstream 5 was a pleasure. Sallie Goddard stretched out in the well-appointed bedroom in the aft fuselage section. Her new boy friend, a beautiful, natural-tanned Filipino surfer, lay beside her. She'd formed a distinct opinion that Filipinos were designed to make anyone forget their troubles and feel oh so good. She stroked him as he slept, tracing his defined pectorals and abs. The lines softened just enough.

Her phone alarm interrupted the bliss of the moment. "Pock, pock, pock." Reality seemed to be knocking on her door. She abandoned the bed and dressed. Soon, they would touch down, and a fully recharged Mayor Sallie would be back on the road to victory.

The landing at the regional Palomar Airport proved uneventful. The mayor, in a short-lived break from the beauty around her, realized she would need to redouble her efforts to get McCracken the property he wanted.

Condos on the bluffs of San E overlooking trillions of gallons of bright blue Pacific would add to his riches. Next time, perhaps he would pop for a bigger plane to take her highness on bigger and better junkets. Perhaps two Filipino surfers.

And for her, the condo project would put a slew of people to work, add a whole lot of new revenues to San E for the mayor to spend, and fortify the workload of the 'hidden' economy—the few hundred Mexican service people who would be needed to service the new residents. "La, la, la, life is sweet," she sang to herself.

Not so fast, Sallie. Her cell phone went off, and it wasn't the good ring tone.

"Now what?" she grumbled through clenched teeth. "They obviously can't run the town without me for a friggin' weekend. Christ on toast."

Mayor Sallie answered the call from her lieutenant, her world deep-sixing in a matter of seconds.

"Where have you been?" Willie gasped. "Do you know what happened? Do you *know* what happened?"

"First off, Wee Willie, you can't go around addressing the mayor as you would an ignored mom. I have been on a brief R and R to none-of-your-business, and I have been doing none-of-your . . . ditto," she scolded.

Before she could ramp up into a more meaningful tirade, Willie interrupted. "Have you seen the paper? Have you seen the freaking *Observer*?"

He obviously had trouble expressing himself under some incorrectly perceived situation, she concluded.

"Why should I bother reading the fucking *San Ernestino Observer* when I was out of town trying to forget that damn place?" she asked. "San E is not my life. It is merely my sustenance, my overly gay home boy."

She tried hard not to feel the big smile she gave herself with that one. "The *Observer* has about as much oomph as a chronically flaccid dick. I don't need to worry about anything with which they might fill their pages. You dig?"

Willie was pissed. He did not like it when the mayor talked down to him while referring to his sexual proclivities. But he had developed a tough enough skin to continue.

"For your information, Treadwell has added a new feature. Yeah. He has added an opinion column and has put someone into the position of writing what the hell is wrong in Happytown. By that, I am, of course, referring to San E. The writer has hit the nail right on the fucking head, and the blood pressure of this little burg, Miss Mayor, has headed due north." Willie could get in his digs, too.

That last comment put Sallie Goddard's Botox to the test. Her brow wrinkled the best it could as she responded, "Okay. Sorry about the gay reference. My driver should have me there in twenty minutes. I'll check it out. We may need to remind Mr. Treadwell of his lowly place in the San E pecking order."

CHAPTER 37

As the sun rose on the proceeding Saturday morning, the sometimes heavy fog began to clear. This was standard operating procedure along the Southern California coast, and the locals just took a little longer getting to work.

The sparse parade from the suburbs, all of three miles at most, took its time down San Ernestino's Main Street. For all of the small towns in America, San E's street was about the same. In length, it was about a mile long and, in width, enough for two lanes of traffic each way. A double yellow stripe down the middle was intended to blockade cars from turning across the street to grab an empty parking spot, but it provided a little extra revenue when the police force caught someone.

Pedestrians lazed down the sidewalks with no apparent place to be in no apparent time frame. In contrast, New Yorkers flowed down the sidewalks at a standard *I've got places to go and people to see* rate. Anytime someone stopped to tie a shoe lace or to gawk at some manifestation of New York's memorable architecture, the flow would instantly split around the offending tourist. Not a second was lost.

Not so in San E. The architecture was comprised mostly of wartime and post-war buildings that were, to say the least, less than memorable. There were never more than a hundred people on foot divided between the two sides of the main street at any one time. Not today.

Chief Connor and his men attempted to contain a disturbance. A number of visibly upset citizens occupied the street in front of City Hall. Some carried signs, calling on the mayor to do her job. The signs indicated that such a doing of job would consist of stopping the increasing loss of employment, city spending on cultural exchanges with foreign cities no-one had ever heard of, and junkets by the mayor to places like France and China. Why did she need to go to southern France to court a trade relationship when San E did not need anything French and vice versa? Everyone knew San E possessed pristine sandy beaches and the best French beaches were covered with smooth stones. And the snails. Ernestinos killed with lethal bait what the gourmet French routinely ate.

The police force struggled with containment, in particular, and crowd control, in general. They had no training in that aspect of police life, because there had been no need in the town's history. Hiring for the cop job was based more on being nice to locals and tourists than on any kind of big city rough stuff.

The boys in blue carried a roll of yellow 'Police Line—Do Not Cross' tape as if believing there might be an application for it somewhere on the scene.

The protesters ignored them.

Chief Connor scanned the crowd for a leader.

The people finally swarmed into a scrum beneath the second-floor balcony of the old brick City Hall Building. They began to shout for the mayor to come out and address their grievances.

Finally, she appeared. In a white smock with a simple gold belt.

"Listen, my friends. I know times have become much harder than anyone anticipated. While we are far better off than those in the larger cities, I realize that it is still painful when you lose a job. When you become fearful of what may come next."

She was actually quite happy about the situation.

She'd decided to use the protest as a pre-emptive measure. When citizens under pressure look to government for solutions, it can be very expensive to the politician who cannot provide. By encouraging them to embrace the grave situation, she could then step in as the savior and show them why they needed government. This age-old tactic always worked. Their hunger for leadership solidified the power at the top. And that would be her.

"The steps we are taking with respect to jobs and spending are being planned as we speak. And just as the morning fog will turn into afternoon sunshine, as it always does, we will come out of these troubled times together."

God, they were stupid, she thought as she continued her election-winning fake smile. The crowd noise died down. The people listened intently, looking up at the pope-in-a-dress figure above. "I will have some good news to tell you in a few days. I can't say anything now, but when I return from Naples, I expect to deliver the news you want to hear."

One of the protesters yelled, "Naples. We don't need you in Italy. We need you here. We don't need to be spending money on political junkets, we need you to spend to create jobs. Now."

She recognized the voice. It was Tom Snow. He had delivered his line as if on cue.

"And we will do just that. I am not going to Naples, Italy, I am going to Naples, Florida." She smiled at them as if they were the great unwashed and she the Second Coming. When she'd finished with them, they would vote on Election Day any way she directed. How wonderful was democracy, she thought. The fact that she was actually going to look for an investment property that would some day serve as her retirement home was just an inconvenient detail.

"I will be meeting with people who can provide us with the means of creating not just jobs, but sustainable employment. I'm asking you to trust me now. Can you do that?" she asked in a manner suggestive of used-car salesmanship.

They bought it. The bloody fools, she thought. I could lead this mentally castrated lot down Elm Street and watch them stream over the bluff in an orderly fashion. That is what they get for watching daytime television. That is what they get for listening to Hollywood's miscreant elite. The people of San Ernestino would go quietly, and she and her fellow thieves would get back to setting up the town for a takeover. She would become mayor for life.

And so it was. The mayor waved her best Elizabethan wave, turned, and retreated into her palace. The crowd, depleted of cause, dispersed and returned home. The Police Chief and his minions scratched their heads.

CHAPTER 38

When Treadwell released the second Dexter Freehand opinion piece, the seed had already been sown. Whoever read the article already knew about the terrible trouble at the national and state levels. They also knew many cities and towns across the country were in dire straits.

Respondent letters to the editor fell into three categories: 1) Those who regularly got network and cable news and already had heard the doom and gloom, 2) those who did not think that any of it effected them personally, and 3) those whose eyes opened wide and said stuff like, "Holy Crap!"

Feedback from the shops and grocery stores, and from the delivery girls and boys, indicated many people anxiously awaited this second installment. They wanted to know how the crisis elsewhere in the country either already did, or would in the future, affect them. When the issue came out, the retail copies—those that were not under subscription, but distributed in retail stores—disappeared quickly.

Thus far, it was good that the editor had shown the experience of his years and had supported Kimbel Stones in his endeavor. Actually, the former received an interesting call that night from a subscriber he'd known for several years.

When she and her husband had visited four years earlier, they'd stopped at the *Observer* and introduced themselves. They told its editor that they had come to San Diego to take their two kids to the famous Zoo and to the Wild Animal Park. On their last day, they decided to drive up the coast. They specifically wanted to show the kids the beauty of the ocean, the waves, and the sandy beaches.

By the time they reached San E, they were sold. They stopped in and asked Treadwell about the beach communities and he, hiding any pretense at objectivity, informed them that San E was the best coastal town anywhere. They asked for a copy of the paper and, using a realtor he recommended, bought their dream house and moved in that summer. He followed their progress and thought that the addition of a teacher and an author were a plus for the community. That night, they sat together pouring over the second Dexter Freehand piece.

They sat on the couch after the kids had been put to bed. He did the honors and, being a writer himself, delivered the article as if it were the mid-segment of a novel—giving emphasis as he new the author had intended.

Editor's note: This is the second installment of articles detailing the current difficult economy. It is best read after reading the first article, which expounded on the nature and depth of the current national crisis. We would appreciate feedback from you regarding your personal plight, should you choose to share it. Please send them to ***editor@thesanernestinoobserver.com****. Thank you, Silas Treadwell, Editor.*

Dear Reader: In the first article, I told you what is going on. I told about what is going on across the country. I told you that no place and no one was being spared. Today, I would like to lay out the many ways that you and your loved ones are being affected.

When we were viciously and surprisingly attacked on September 11, our president asked us to do our mourning, but then go on with our normal routines. And the nation followed.

We all went on about our business, and the anti-terror war became a droning in the background. In previous wars, however, America had gone to what was called a wartime footing. People went into the services, their work moved to factories that made wartime materials, and everyone participated in the war effort.

Today, as we try to get on with our lives, other Americans are being bowled over with the awful truth. They are losing jobs, they are losing health coverage, they are being thrown out of their homes. Now, sadly, San E is beginning to feel what others have felt. Our citizens are starting to realize that the government that promises to get them out of this crisis is the same government that caused it in the first place.

Sarah Parker is an elderly lady, who lives on the north side of San E. She has lived here all her life. Her home is the home of her parents and where Sarah grew up. She went to school at Franklin Elementary, and then on to the local junior and senior high schools. Most people know her as the woman who worked in the local library and who rang the Salvation Army bell during the holidays. She is a good woman by all accounts.

But now, like so many people, her sunset years have turned from golden to dark. Her pension from the city library has been reduced to the point she cannot pay her mortgage. She can no longer afford the medicine she needs as the Federal, state, and local assistance programs have slipped into bankrupt status. She has received an eviction notice from the mortgage holder. Her life has turned from heaven to hell. She is one of us.

We can all pitch in and help Sarah, but that is not why I am writing. Sarah's problems are becoming everyone's problems. Others just like you face unaffordable housing and health expenses. As people lose jobs right here in San E, the city's tax base is crumbling. Our businesses are closing with increasing rapidity. The city itself is on a path to bankruptcy. That's right, bankruptcy. City Hall has begun issuing IOU's. It is late on payments to contractors, and its credit rating has been lowered to junk status. The pension fund for city employees has been devastated by the crisis on Wall Street and will run out of money in just a few years.

You will remember I said earlier that Sarah's story is our story. No one is immune. The government that we hope will get us out of this severe situation is itself inept. But there is good news. We can pull together. We, the good citizens of San E, can not only make a difference, we can solve the problem right now. In my third and final article, I will tell you exactly what we need to do.

Respectfully & rightfully pissed off,
Dexter Freehand, Citizen.

CHAPTER 39

When the *Observer* came out on Sunday, it was like none before it. The cover did not have the usual leads to major inside content. It had only the masthead and a big color headshot of Mayor Sallie Goddard. It was a photo never seen before in print. In place of the constant sardonic smile of the politician, this shot showed her with a countenance of meanness that would have made the devil proud.

Inside, there were no advertisements and no classifieds in the back. There was only the final commentary by the alter ego of Kimbel R. Stones. This is what he said,

> *Editor's note: The following is the third article in the Dexter Freehand series, regarding the very trying times that affect the country as a whole, our grand state, and, as you have seen, our own beautiful town. It is the third after the initial article, which defined the problem, and the second article on how it affects all of us. This article may make good sense on its own, but as the last in the series, it strikes hard at what must be done. If you have not already done so, please find a copy of the first two articles so you can get the full*

impact. I can safely say that your very future is at stake and will, without control, blow in the prevailing ill wind if you neglect Mr. Freehand's warnings and sage advice. As always, please send us your responses to the articles as well as your personal observances and situations. Send them to ***editor@thesanernestinoobserver.com****. Thank you, Silas Treadwell, Editor.*

Dear Reader: It is in the nature of most people to be trusting. We trust our parents. We trust the police. We trust the news. But most of all, we trust the people we elect to determine what needs to be done and then to do it. That applies to all issues for which we endow them with responsibility. We expect them to be among the best of us. We expect them to use their intelligence, their knowledge, their skills, and their talents to foresee and deflect serious problems and to solve those that get through.

We suffer the sometimes painful election process so that we can have it over and return to the things that matter to us most. It includes taking care of ourselves and our loved ones. It includes work, play, vacation, relaxation—all those necessary and pleasurable activities that make life itself a wonderful experience.

So what happens when our faith is unjustified? What happens when the rewards that our elected leaders seek are completely out of concert with our expectations? What happens when greed for undeserved and excessive wealth comes before the hardworking citizens of this town? What happens when the lust for power supersedes the welfare of our children? It's simple. We lose. We all lose.

We lose big when a leader satisfies her own selfishness and then lies to us that everything is being done that can be done. We lose big when a developer bribes that elected leader for uncalled-for zoning changes and special favors. Perhaps bribe is too harsh a word. Perhaps I should use the politically correct term: donation.

If you have already read my first two articles, then you know that I am not talking about some corrupt mega-city back East. You know that I am not talking about any of America's poorer states. No, I am talking about our own piece of paradise. I am talking about San Ernestino. This San Ernestino. Our San Ernestino.

We are rewarding bad behavior when we get so complacent that elections become walk-through events. The speeches are meaningless as are the clapping and smiling and banners and confetti that go along with the whole absurd process. We want good behavior, but we reward bad. It is as simple as that. And then we go on with our lives and are taken completely by surprise when politicians are exposed to us for the criminals they are. And then we are disgusted and angry. And then we do it all over again.

Scientists call it inertia. They say that an object that is moving in a certain direction and at a certain speed will continue to do so until acted upon by some other object or force. We should not be surprised that the physical laws that govern all existence apply to politics, as well. The only way we can correct the problems we face is to apply our force, as citizens of this town, to the inert object that is City Hall, and to move it once and for all in the direction that we have wanted all along.

It should occur to you all by now that voting, as our forefathers proscribed for us, is not enough. We must sift through the smoke screens, find the factual evidence, and then spur ourselves and our neighbors to make this right. Make it right now; make it right for the future. The impromptu actions by a few rightfully concerned citizens last week sent the first warning message. It has been ignored. I am calling on everyone who can possibly do so to come to City Hall tomorrow at 9 A.M., bring signs, bring your children. We have had enough.

Respectfully & rightfully pissed off,
Dexter Freehand, Citizen.

• • •

The paper was delivered to the usual subscriber base, plus it was stacked in all of the stores, free for the taking. It disappeared so fast and the response was so intensely favorable, Silas Treadwell ran a second printing. And he continued printing until his supply of paper was gone. The phone rang off the hook, and all he heard was outrage. He received calls that people were coming in from neighboring towns just to see what was causing the commotion.

Treadwell had to admit, the piece was dynamite. It flowed, and it bit hard. He considered the greater good that this might do and then brushed it aside long enough to congratulate himself again for the good hire. He muttered, "*Damn, I'm good.*" three or four times for effect. Then, he went about rush-ordering more paper. For the first time in a long, long while, he smelled blood. And it smelled good.

CHAPTER 40

Monday morning opened on a sight that was not pretty. The largest crowd by far had gathered in front of San Ernestino's City Hall. But it was not merely the size, it was who had been added. There were now kids, grownups, white hairs, and, driving up in a battery-powered wheelchair, Quentin Han. The man who liked to keep to his own affairs and leave the protesting to others was the center of everyone's attention.

Han rode to the front of the crowd and spun the chair to face them. Someone called for the crowd to quiet down. Mr. Han had something to say.

"What I am about to do, I never would have imagined," he began. "My wife cannot be here. She is still hospitalized. I agonized at having to leave her, even though she slept and was expected to do so for several hours. My place is by her side. Please, fellow citizens ... a moment of prayer for her."

The crowd hushed to total silence.

Han finished a few minutes later with, "Amen."

The people repeated, then hung on his every word.

"I am not a speaker, I am a listener. I have read the works of Dexter Freehand, and I have looked around. He is right in every way. In the end, the government is us. Those people we elect are mere representatives."

Quentin Han paused while they digested his thoughts.

"It is we who place them most undeservedly on pedestals, and it is we who afford them respect that they seldom earn. We are being betrayed. We are being betrayed by corruption. We are being betrayed by incompetence. We must make our feelings known by our numbers and by our collective voice."

The crowd in its entirety produced applause, hoots, hollers, thumbs up, and high fives. The sleepy town of San Ernestino had awakened.

Peering down from a second floor window, the mayor displayed her mastery of the four-letter word to anyone who would listen.

"I'll show those little people why I am up here, and they are down there," she hissed. "I'll show that fat-headed little foreigner why he should have remained a listener, and not one who stirs up what is best left alone. I am not just the duly-elected mayor of this village, I am its queen." With that, she walked out onto the balcony and, to various catcalls and boos, began to speak.

"I know that you are upset, my friends. I also know that our wonderful newspaper, the *Observer*, has gone off the reservation and lowered itself to opinionated musings that are not the least bit helpful under these trying times."

The crowd had grown from its original sixty people to ninety. Whenever the mayor stopped talking, the catcalls and boos commenced anew. Undaunted, she continued in her mayoral manor.

"Everything is under control. The local effects of the national economic crises are being overblown and everything is in the process of being addressed by me and my capable staff. Must I remind you that it is you who put me in charge? I intend to use my authority to lead the city to a more solvent place."

A fervent buzz broke out amongst the people. Rambunctious at first, it dissipated after a few minutes.

With that, she waved at the crowd and disappeared back inside.

Members of the crowd remained unsatisfied. The conversations among them continued at a moderate level as they processed the mayor's remarks.

As they began to disperse, one man called out, "Everybody. The final Freehand article is our call to action. Make sure your family and friends read all three. I can see by the mayor's attitude, we will have to make changes this coming election."

All heads nodded up and down.

"I've got copies for everyone."

The citizens filed by and, copies in hand, they departed.

CHAPTER 41

The hammer came down on City Hall. The lights on the second floor burned bright long after the sun had bid adieu. The mayor moved to restore calm among her staff.

"Things are going to be just fine. I will deal with the *Observer*'s opinionated tirade in due time. This is much fucking ado about absolutely fucking nothing. What does the *Observer* know about anything? It's a tired old rag that runs a few ads and fills the rest with marshmallow stories. Substance is an unknown around that place. The nerve."

She hoped, however, her cronies and subordinates missed the clenching of jaw that came over her on this particular subject. How dare this 'People's Republic' *Observer* have an opinion, and how dare that over-the-hill editor, Silas Treadwell, disguise the byline? How the hell was she supposed to have McCracken's latest thug beat the crap out of the son-of-a-bitch author of that editorial piece.

She was so close. So close to having it all her way. She slammed both fists down onto her desk in frustration. What to do? What to do?

That question was answered with a call. Incoming. Willie Sample burst through the double doors, out of breath. Given that he had only travelled fifteen feet, something serious was afoot.

"Jesus Christ," he yelled. "Mama, you gotta pick up on One." He paused for effect. "Somebody claiming to have the goods on the opinion guy. Name. Rank. Serial number. The whole schlemiel."

"Stop the juvenile panting and raving. Bottom line, Willie, or I will use my fucking girl scout knife to turn your love life into gumbo meat." She obviously did not want to play with the subject.

Willie tried to calm down, but unsuccessfully. "Insider. Got the goods. Wants to meet."

"Put him on. I'll decide if this is real." Sallie had enough experience with bullshit tattletale crap.

"Yeah. Right away," said Willie. "Oh, it's not a he," he added. "Female."

Before she punched in the '1' and took the call, she started to feel a bit of a rush. She mused. What if this is really manna from heaven? She drew a breath, held it, and let it out slowly. "Let's see…"

The mayor waited until Willie closed her office doors, then answered with the usual, "Hello, Mayor Goddard here. To whom am I speaking?"

The party on the other end stayed quiet at first, but then spoke just above a whisper. "We'll keep this simple. I know for absolute certain who the mystery opinion writer for the *Observer* is. If you are interested, I have but one non-negotiable demand. Interested?"

Yes, the speaker was decidedly female. Sallie could not place the voice. The whisper gave away nothing. She played her first card. "Look, we get a lot of junk calls, claiming everything from seeing God down at the beach to predicting the next apocalypse. Why should I believe you?"

"It's simple. I have discovered the identity of Dexter Freehand. But first, my solitary demand is this. If by some chance you determine who I am, you will reveal it to no one. You will happily agree because

I have something on you that will pretty much write off your career betraying the public trust if you don't."

Mayor Sallie let the dig slide. Time to get to the substance. "You have fifteen seconds."

"The meat I have on you is seventeen-year-old meat. The kind that flies to offshore islands with older women. Jail time, sweetheart."

Sallie's heart started into overdrive.

How could she know?

Was this something McCracken cooked up?

Did that little brown bastard kiss and tell?

Whatever, the mayor realized she had to go all in. Too late to turn back now.

"And?" she said, her voice rising at the end.

"I'll say this once. The man writing the opinion pieces for the *Observer* is…" and she gave the name.

"Holy Jesus Christ," breathed the mayor. "That son-of-a-bitch." Sallie had fallen out of character, the news hit her so hard. "That fucking sit-and-listen new hire. Lives with the Hans. It's fucking revenge. He found the link between old Johnny M and me, and now he's sticking it right up my ass."

Her eyes had defocused to a blur as she rocked back in her chair.

"I owe you," she finally said. "If I ever find you out, just name your poison, honey." Sallie hung up.

The caller hung up, too. She was not happy with herself as she ran her fingers through her hair. The emotions had turned severe for her to fall this low. In one way, she felt satisfaction. In another, she felt disgusted with herself. Who the hell was she, anyway?

CHAPTER 42

The three men stood in silence for a few moments. First Advisor Raspi and SVR head Yuri Orlov didn't intend to be the first to speak. They awaited the next pearl of wisdom from the third most powerful man on Earth, the same man who stood before them in his favorite, faded, red and yellow bathrobe.

"We had something in the old days. We controlled it all. The country. The people. Our influence pervaded the world. And then it disappeared. Years it took, but it seemed over night." Vladimir turned to his First Advisor. "I want it back, Raspi." He turned toward his foreign intelligence chief. "I want it back, Yuri."

The Russian head of state's chief aide was adamant. "Vladimir—you told me to use that rather than your surname—what you are considering is impossible. Worse than that, it's suicidal. You cannot restore communism in this country in order to obtain absolute power. The pain of the 70-year soviet worker's paradise persists in the nation's elderly. And now that they can speak, they pass the horror of it down to their offspring, like so much family lore. Except, it's all true."

"Raspi, Raspi, Raspi. It's not the ideology I require, it's the power. Now that I have corroboration that the czarina's granddaughter is alive, I have the perfect solution. I will rehabilitate the image of that royalty, and elevate her to Dowager Empress, restoring the czarist crown."

"Fine. So she's this empress, and you're still president of Russia. How does that help?"

"I must find a way, perhaps by decree, that I am of the Romanov bloodline."

"That could be done," Raspi contemplated. "Fake DNA."

The president scored an epiphany. His jaw dropped. "Better yet. Simply have her adopt me. In any event, I become Czar Vladimir." He turned to the SVR chief. "Yuri, what are your thoughts. Candor, please."

Yuri felt as if he'd entered the Russian version of the Twilight Zone. He could almost hear the handle being pushed on a large toilet, and the three of them being flushed into an eternal sewer. He had to speak his mind.

"Candor you shall have. You have lost your mind, my president. Do you think for a moment that those in the Kremlin would stand by? And what of elections? All that would have to disappear. And human rights. What few that exist would vanish. The power structure would not allow it."

"You are perhaps correct in your assessment." He turned to his advisor. "I need to speak to Yuri alone. Please wait in my quarters."

Raspi did as ordered. Yuri Orlov had just stepped pretty far. With his own scalp still intact, retreat seemed a good idea.

As soon as the door clicked shut behind his advisor, Vladimir turned to Orlov.

"Your SVR intelligence has told me that the Chinese may have developed a special bomb. A radiation-free nuclear device that is small, yet displaces the power of millions of tons of dynamite. And somehow, with no radiation after. It would be perfect to dismantle the entirety of the elite, while leaving most of Moscow intact."

Orlov rolled his eyes. "I feel like I've entered—what was that program I mentioned?"

"The Twilight Zone." Vladimir had all episodes in a boxed set.

"Yes." The older SVR man plowed fingers through a rapidly disappearing hairline.

"And I shall blame the Muslim Chechens. It's perfect. Unless, of course, you have a better plan."

"A one-way move to the French Riviera seems a better plan."

"There's something unrelated. I have learned that the KGB archives not released to the public show that the former American president utilized our assassination technique. Kill the target such that everyone who might think of committing a similar offence is convinced they will die and their killers will never be punished."

"Please, Vladimir. More detail."

"An American stole many millions. He moved to Switzerland and later received a presidential pardon and, coincidentally, donated a large sum to the presidential library of that very man who gave the pardon."

"There is no killing in that story."

"It signified the mood. A woman refused to testify against the same president and his wife, knowing that she would receive wealth if she remained silent, and a pardon if convicted. It merely required that her legal troubles be resolved before the president's term ended."

"What if she'd talked?"

"Another individual, a man, decided to do just that. He sought immunity before he could be prosecuted. He was murdered in such a manner that everyone knew the official suicide determination had been manufactured. In the White House. In the Oval Office."

"I see. So no one else talked."

"Tell me, Orlov. Would you kill for me?"

"I'm your head of foreign intelligence. Do you ask this of me to prove my loyalty?"

"I'm vulnerable. You know of my proclivity for youthful males. In fact, it was you who devised the disinformation campaign. I prove my masculinity by appearing on horseback, shirtless, with rifles, even the anti-gay campaign. Brilliant. I was the man's man. No, my friend, your loyalty is not in question. I need to see if you can do it. Here."

He lifted a Makarov semi-automatic pistol from a desk drawer, verified its readiness, and handed it to the other man.

He buzzed his administrative assistant in the outer chamber.

"I wish a hot tea … with vodka."

"*Da*," came the response.

Orlov's brow furrowed. His left eyebrow lifted, as was the norm when he stressed.

"You want me to …"

"Yes. Kill him."

The other man produced nothing more than a blank, unseeing stare.

"Yuri, I have trusted you with my deepest and darkest secrets. I feel most vulnerable. As I described to you earlier, my direction is about to take a major change. This is your final test."

A knock.

"Enter."

The middle-aged man pushed a samovar cart inside, shutting the door behind him. He wheeled it to the desk, handing the Russian president a cup of tea.

"Orlov has something for you."

The assistant turned.

The sound of the gunshot, deafening in the vibrant quarters, caused both men to recoil. The single shot blew a hole in the victim's chest sending blood in every direction.

The door burst open. Guards stormed in, automatic rifles ready.

The blood-spattered president pointed at Orlov. "He's got a gun!"

In seconds, the SVR head's bullet-riddled body struck the floor.

The president, in a pretense of controlled excitement, synopsized the moment.

“He killed my man, who’d stepped in front of me. A hero. Get the body of this traitor out of my sight. And get housekeeping.”

The guards shouldered their weapons, and had the Orlov corpse gone in less than twenty seconds. The lead man, thankful that the body wasn’t his, closed the door behind, and put in the cleanup request over his communication device.

Proud of his treachery, Vladimir stepped through the door into his quarters.

• • •

“You don’t approve?” the Russian president asked First Advisor Raspi.

“He knew, and has known for some time, far too much. I believe he was dead when he walked in.”

“Not about him, about my plan.”

“Let’s revisit. To be clear.”

“We make her the monarch, Raspi. She has the credentials, the blood line.”

“Not a chance. The upper and lower houses of the Federal Assembly, not to mention our Supreme Court, would never stand for it. All of their corruption would be unveiled by this woman, this czarina. They would have to work for a living.”

“I have an idea, my friend.”

“Your idea—whatever it is—could see us both being shot!”

A moment passed.

“What is this idea?”

“I call it my Nuclear Option.”

From Vladimir’s bed chambers, Raspi had eavesdropped on the president’s conversation with the SVR head. He now followed the mental pathway. Convene the legislature. Then, acquire and utilize one of the Chinese mini-bombs.

Nuclear.

CHAPTER 43

Stones spent his last hours that day at the *Observer* in the morgue. It wasn't to dive into some last minute researching now that the rest of the building had headed home, but rather to reflect in peace. About something that occurred when he'd first regained consciousness after the Diomede fiasco. Something extremely troubling.

He recalled what the rescuing CIA operative with the comic book sounding code name, Magic Man, had shown him in his *safe hospital* room.

It seemed the hunter's red and black patterned flannel shirt supplied by the NSA had been coated in a supple plastic—to hold in body heat and keep out the bitter Bering Sea cold. Or so he'd been told.

The intelligence operative stood close to the bed and ripped open the fabric to reveal a grid of very fine wires.

"They probably transmit heat," Stones had mumbled.

"Not so. The grid's a powerful antenna."

"It must be for some kind of heat transfer. It did something. It helped keep me from freezing to death. Of course, the bullet didn't help."

Magic Man then plucked the buttons from the shirt front, snatched a doctor's reflex-testing hammer from a table, and pounded them until each broke.

All but one yielded a tiny battery. The last gave up a miniscule computer chip.

"The batteries powered this controller chip," he pointed. "The grid antenna was there to supply an incoming signal to the chip."

Stones, peering through a slit in his temperature-stabilizing wrap, shook his head. "Bullshit!"

Within a minute, the CIA man stood outside stuffing the pieces into a snow bank, visible in full through the window.

He returned, then punched in a number on his Smartphone.

Fwoomp! went the shirt.

The mini-blast sent snow in all directions.

Stones just stared as blown globs of white lost adhesion and fell from the window.

Fascinated, he realized he'd been just one cell or satellite phone call from being betrayed.

"I know what you're thinking," the operative said. "The answer to your questions is NO. This operation was so hot, your people back in Washington couldn't allow you to get captured."

"They probably just grabbed it up, not knowing its lethal potential," Stones rationalized.

"Not possible. They keep these in a special place. Under lock and key. I know."

He'd closed his eyes, then heard the door close. Magic Man was gone.

His mind returned to the current circumstance.

Kimbel had more pressing troubles to resolve. His mind snapped back to the present. He went to work, knowing that he needed some damning evidence to shake up City Hall and he thought an end-around tactic might be his best ploy. He called a number in his little black book that was not a potential date. This individual excelled at tracking down information in a place where a lot of people did that.

Kimbel provided the name of the local developer, indicating he needed intel on the workers he paid. All of them. He needed a dossier on anyone who'd done time, been in the armed services, served in law enforcement, or in any way had a background conducive to the kind of activity carried out on the Han residence.

He tried to get into some other work, but the thought of nailing McCracken and his hired gun made changing focus impossible. Forty-five minutes later, the phone rang. He tapped the decryption button.

"Mr. Kimbel, Sir, this is me," said the caller. "One Ezekiel Zablowski at your service."

"Drop the honorifics, Zeke. This one is off the books."

Stones had known Zeke for a long, long time. The Zablowskis took sympathy on his bachelor status and frequently asked him over to share homemade enchiladas. Of Hispanic ethnicity, Zeke's wife cooked the meanest enchiladas on planet Earth.

"What happened, you forget the parameters?" joked Kimbel.

"No. No. No. I've got your intel, and it's smokin' hot. Can I go?"

"Go," said Kimbel, knowing full well he had just turned on the spigot and would struggle to get in another word.

"Well, I went to McCracken's payroll data and his tax data and, unless he paid someone on the sly—you know, with no social and stuff—it all wiggles down to just one guy. Dude that goes by the name, Beener. I swear to God. Beener. Dude did incendiaries in the Army. I also got a sheet on him from law enforcement. Seems he's pulled similar pranks before. And always in the business region of boss man McCracken. He never got pulled down for any of it, though. It seems things were settled out of court."

"For Chrissakes, Zeke. I need details."

"The out of court episodes involved some 911 calls with descriptions that fit old Beener, but no one ever went the distance and pressed charges. That's how these cats keep on keepin' on. They figure this is their livelihood and so they heavily encourage their victims and witnesses to think about their own futures. That's why we've got so many of these assholes around. Oh, the full name as far as I can tell is Beener Jackman. Ring a bell?" Zeke asked rhetorically. "McCracken lists him as having Foreman status and pays him large bonuses. I couldn't find any indication from my worldwide resources to indicate that old Beener had any of the usual tickets the Construction Foreman handle requires. No journeyman status. Not even any apprenticeships."

Finally, Kimbel got in a few words. "Okay. That's enough for me to get started on," he said as he pulled Zeke's chain.

"What 'get started'?" complained Zeke. "Any more and I'll have to charge you my exorbitant rates. Hell, I know all I'll get is an IOU. But since you will probably bomb out on the credit check, it won't be a problem."

Before Kimbel could sincerely thank the man, Zeke had one more thought he wanted to share.

"It does tickle me that these supposedly big-time crooks like McCracken use their regular payroll for this type of stuff. They're so up there, they think, that they'll never get caught. So they might just as well get the tax deduction for the expense. Once you're done with the reaming of the asshole process, you might want to turn him over to the IRS. I've got a number if you decide to go that route."

"You know how these things are, Zeke. We'll see how this plays out. I do owe you big time, but I may need more. So start a tab," Kimbel rang off.

Thanks to Zeke, he had a name. All he needed now was a solid link between McCracken and the mayor on the development deal. Something that would hook the mayor to Beener through McCracken.

When he had that, it was ashes, ashes … we all fall down.

CHAPTER 44

The current day had been a rough one. Kimbel Stones swung his BMW into the Motel 6 parking lot. He was tired to the point of exhaustion. Back early, he reasoned Susanna would not be in their room, and he'd be able to rest a bit before she returned.

Things didn't begin well. His key card resisted his every effort to unlock the door. He persisted, feeling even more worn when it finally relented.

For a moment, he wanted to be able to toss his hat onto a rack across the room. Like the fabled James Bond. Alas, he'd never worn a hat.

He closed the door behind, but left off the chain in anticipation of Susanna arriving in about half an hour. His fingers went to his shirt buttons, just not in the cool, sexy manner she did.

Then, a sound.

From the bathroom.

Stones glanced over to see that the door was ajar.

"Hmmm," he thought out loud. "She's already here. In the shower. I was so dilapidated, I didn't even see her car in the lot." The thought switched gears. "I will surprise her."

With that, he removed the remainder of his garments, silently slid past the door, closing it behind him.

Usually, she sang in the shower. Not this time. The frosted glass gave up her feminine figure, but not much more.

He stepped closer, unable to suppress a smile.

He opened the shower door.

There, before him, an hourglass figure and blonde tresses.

Not Susanna's figure. Not Susanna's hair.

Dumbfounded, he stammered, "Who are you?"

The young woman stepped from under the spray and retrieved an institutional white towel draped over the shower stall. With a smile that would have undressed him had that been necessary, she dabbed the towel between her breasts.

"Please come in."

The woman was pretty, but pure business. She stood about an inch shorter than Susanna.

His eyes followed the towel's dangling end to the floor.

She moved it sideways.

In her right hand, a Makarov semiautomatic was leveled at his private parts.

"*Seychas!*"

Stones had a smattering vocabulary with respect to foreign languages. He knew the imperative for NOW in Russian.

He looked her up and down, then examined her face as he stepped in.

"You're not the cleaning lady."

She shook her head.

"You have the European Slavic look, but the accent seems off."

"My parents moved east. Past Siberia."

He thought. "Sakhalin?"

"*Da*," she responded. "Korsakovsky District. The town of Korsakov. South of the capital."

"I don't suppose my room card let me into the wrong room?"

"No."

"I—"

"We will skip the small talk, as you say. That item you stole. From our base on the island. Where is it at this moment? And who has had it?"

Her statement blew beyond profound in what it revealed. She knew about his operation on Big Diomede. Worse, she knew what he'd taken. And likely, what it contained.

His search for words, any words, stopped short.

Behind him, the bathroom door burst open.

"Hi, honey," Susanna cried out. "I'm…"

Her jaw dropped full open.

She'd heard the shower running, and, like Stones and for the same intent, stood stark naked.

Having few options, he covered himself with his hands.

"What's this?" She gestured at the Russian. "One last fling before you propose?"

She was good at staying cool and calm. Her trademark. But this was new. She'd allowed herself to trust. To be vulnerable. A requisite for love. Her eyes welled up. Mascara ran down her cheeks.

"Join us," Valya said, more a command than a request.

Wiping away the wetness to clear her vision, Susanna's eyes blazed at the woman.

"I don't—"

Valya, who'd re-hidden her firearm when the door had opened, drew it from behind the towel. She motioned a hesitating Susanna inside the shower stall.

"*Seychas!*"

Stones wanted to take deep breaths. He couldn't. He'd gotten involved with someone, forgetting his recent, excessively dangerous past. Now, his someone very special was in mortal danger. Thanks to him.

He translated. "It means—"

"Now," said Susanna. "Russian for immediately."

Stones, confident that he'd gotten the handle on everything up to about twenty minutes before, now felt like the Lone Ranger without Tonto.

The Russian, who had to be an SVR operative, was not just a 'blonde bombshell' in appearance, but one in the more insidious and dangerous sense of the characterization.

And now, Susanna came across sounding like her equal.

Valya pointed the weapon back at Stones' crotch. "Try nothing or..."

The movement was just enough.

Susanna lunged into the Russian.

The blast from the weapon deafened in the confined space.

Stones went down.

Both women glanced at the man on the shower floor.

Water spray pecked at his grimacing face and wounded body.

The liquid headed for the drain morphed red.

Both women needed Stones alive for very different reasons.

Back to the moment, Valentina pushed with her weapon hand, and pulled with her free hand. She had to eliminate the other.

Susanna, typically elegant and graceful, held the pistol at bay while grasping the flex-connected shower wand.

Two quick wraps around the Russian's neck, and the battle tide changed.

Valentina dropped the Makarov. She fought the hose cutting off her air with both hands.

A losing battle. As her opponent fought for purchase, Susanna stepped in a puddle of soap residue.

Her feet slid from beneath.

She fell, her hands still locked on the wand.

Snap! came the ugly sound.

Landing hard on Stones, Susanna glanced up to see the source of the wicked noise.

Valentina Kummonova. Head twisted at a lethal angle. Dead.

The battle over, Susanna knelt, grabbed the white towel that lay soaked on the stall floor, and pushed it hard on Stones' wound, lest he bleed to death.

She caught her breath after a few seconds, positioned his hand over the wound, and ordered, "Hold this. I'll be right back."

In the bedchamber, Susanna located her oversized purse. She withdrew several items, ran back into the bathroom, and set them next to Stones.

One item, a surgeon's optical scope—with a long-nose plier-like attachment—she used to retrieve the slug lodged in his thigh.

He had stuffed a piece of towel into his mouth to muffle any outcries during a medical procedure that lasted less than a minute.

"When we take someone down, almost never does an autopsy find the slug . . . with its markings and all. We attend a class for this."

"A class?" He waited a second. "We?"

"No, no. What just happened here?"

"I suppose an explanation of my own might be appropriate at this point."

She turned to look at him dead on. "Do you think?"

Stones retold her everything, filling in all the blanks. About all of his work at the NSA. What he'd left out about the covert op on Big Diomede. About the intelligence device he'd extracted, during a blizzard and under fire, from the Russian Federation fortress. Everything.

After digesting it all, Susanna let out a long, slow breath. "So much for Dexter Freehand, the newbie star reporter for the San Ernestino *Observer*. What the hell are you doing *here*?"

Stones didn't answer. He just peered directly into her eyes.

She nodded. She knew what he was saying without words. What he asked.

"Yeah, well, I guess I did show some non-advertising-executive skills just then."

He didn't move. Not even an eyelash.

"I suppose everyone has a back story, Kimbel. One that doesn't match up with the one everybody hears."

He waited.

She glanced around. Then, up at the dead Russian.

"I guess we're alone. Enough. So, here's the rest of mine."

CHAPTER 45

When Kimbel awoke in his Motel 6 room several hours later, he sat up to clear his vision. It was still blurred from the night before. He could hear rain outside and opened the blinds to let in some natural light. As he did, the drops splashing against the window pane reminded him of his own life: hitting a hard object and dispersing without control.

He turned to see if Susanna was awake. She was gone. It was bad enough his life had spun out of control, now he worried she might do something. He needed to find her. Somehow.

First, he had a little something to take care of. The body in the shower.

The NSA did not dispose of bodies as part of normal operations.

That wouldn't be a problem, he told himself.

Stones called the fixer. He called Zeke.

"Hello, old friend."

"It's really good to see you once again."

"I just love using the Eric Clapton lines. Someday I'll shake hands with you again for real."

"What's up?"

"I've got a lump. Not in my throat. Elsewhere."

He could imagine Zeke nodding up and down with a knowing smile. He'd been here before.

"Got just the thing."

He provided a long, nonsensical number. Upper-case. Lower-case. Numbers. Special characters. Nothing seemed to be in any particular order.

"Give me a sec."

The fixit man went offline for just over five minutes.

He returned.

"They'll drop off the container in thirty. Give you two hours. Be back. Pick up. Done."

"Keep this quiet. Don't let the suits know. Especially my suits. I need this to be a surprise."

"No problem."

"T H X."

The line went dead.

It occurred just the way Zeke Zablowski said it would. Stones took the sturdy, reinforced box, removed the roll of plastic packing tape inside, added the body, sealed it, and printed the extraordinary, eighteen-character tracking number on the label. Stones knew that there would be no signatures either way.

In precisely two hours, the transporter, who looked as if he'd played fullback at Notre Dame, returned. He helped Stones tote the hard-sided, aircraft quality container to the truck.

"Jeez," the man remarked as they hefted it inside. "What y'all got in here, a body?"

"Now, that's funny," Stones replied with a smile.

Uncharacteristically, the UPS man and his big brown truck tore out of the Motel 6 parking lot, leaving a pair of black strips in his wake.

Kimbel Stones felt he had washed his hands—in all senses of the words—of the Valentina Kummonova affair.

He attempted to restrain a smile at a mental picture of his NSA superior's countenance upon opening the box. Pure justice. Andrew Scott had sent him to the Diomede Islands in the first place.

"Oh, look. A body," he would say. "For my birthday."

Stones chuckled at the irony. Yes, the package would be delivered the next day. And, yes, that happened to be Andrew's birthday.

As he sequestered himself back inside the room, his mind shifted to a very special woman.

CHAPTER 46

Kimbel sat alone in his motel room. The blinds were drawn. He had been in a situation like this before. You look. You try to see, but you just stare. Your mind goes into lockdown mode out of self defense.

His phone rang. He recognized the voice.

"Hello, Silas."

"Just finished talking to the mayor."

"I think she has you on speed dial now."

"Not good, Kimbel. She knows."

"Knows?"

"Dexter Freehand. She knows."

"There goes my magic. How?"

"She didn't say. She threatened to expose you, unless …"

"Don't tell me. She wants you to stop the series and, perhaps, say something nice about her."

"That's about it. Think about it. I know you. You'll come up with something. Sorry to bum out your day."

"Yeah, it was going so well."

Editor Treadwell rung off.

Stones slipped into mental torment.

If he had only stayed in D.C. If they had just said *No* to his request for a leave of absence. If… if… if.

Kimbel liked rum. Bacardi 151. Seventy-five-point-five percent alcohol. It was his drink. That and just about anything mixed with it did him just fine. With it, he could really get loose. At this moment, he did not want loose. Just numb.

A knock at the door. He ignored it. Unfortunately, whoever was outside refused to go away. Hum. Hum. Hum. Finally, he issued a "Come in—add to my misery."

The door was not locked. It was not even closed. If a robber came in, maybe he would put an end to Kimbel's funk. He felt he had not done the Hans the least bit of good. He had, in fact, brought catastrophe upon them. He had encouraged them to fight back, nearly getting them killed.

The door opened to reveal the last person he expected to see.

Susanna.

"I came to check up on you. Silas got us all together and told us about your alter ego role. That you were Dexter Freehand. And how someone ratted you out to City Hall. I'm sorry."

She appeared to be genuinely sorry, but Kimbel could not tell. He just leaned back on the couch and continued to stare at the wall picture that must have come from the 99-cent store. It depicted a cowboy on a horse. There was nothing nor anyone else in the picture. Alone. Like Kimbel.

She tilted her head back and shut her eyes.

He knew. She felt it.

Before she could even think, her mind, like her eyes, snapped to black.

When she fainted, she did not see Kimbel move with the speed and agility reserved for a cat.

He caught her just before she hit the floor.

• • •

A short while later, Susanna regained consciousness. She found herself lying on the couch, Kimbel seated beside her, a wet washcloth in his hand. He had tried the age-old cold wet cloth on the forehead remedy, and it had worked.

"I apologize for the ubiquitous institutional white washcloth. It is standard fare in all of these better motels," he said.

She smiled faintly. "Thanks, Kimbel. I'm sorry for the entrance. It wasn't my best. I've got something to …"

Kimbel cut her off. "Look, just rest a bit. You went down like a sack of… well, marshmallows," he said, not wanting to refer to her and a sack of potatoes in the same sentence. That had gotten him in trouble before.

"No," she said. "It's why I'm here. Really. Please, just listen." He nodded and she continued. "When I first saw you, I thought, okay, things are looking up. I'm getting into my 30's and my clock seems to keep moving faster and faster. Then, at work, I saw you see her. It's not her fault although I wish it was. She's not even competition. She's just… Luisa."

Susanna seemed to be rambling on about something. But he knew to listen rather than comment until she got where she needed to go.

"It upset me, anyway. Isn't jealousy fun? It became my duty as a jilted woman, even though you and I had absolutely nothing going on, to balance the books."

She spoke softly, but the direction of her comments began to take shape.

"I found out early on about your Dexter Freehand, alter ego thing. How it was you who was anonymously commenting rather strongly on the nature of governance in this little burg. How the public just wants to trust in the people they elect to public office, and how that is never enough. How, unfettered by public input and outcry, these political types, who owe their existence to the people, manage to turn away from them, ignore incompetence, and sell the powers of their offices to the highest bidder. Like the other people of this town, I read those pieces you wrote. Then I reread them."

She stopped for a second, closed her eyes, and when she reopened them. "It was me, Kimbel. I did it," she said as she teared up.

"No . . ."

"God forgive me. It was me who called the mayor. It was me. And I'm so not proud of what I did. That's how she knew. That's how they outed you to Silas."

She began to sob, her hands covering her face.

Kimbel sat still.

Another time, he would have been angry. He would have thrown her out. He might have gotten physical in a very bad way.

But not tonight. His numbness was the catalyst. Not much of anything was going to change that.

"Susanna. Don't say any more. Get some sleep. We'll talk when we've both had some rest."

He gently picked her up, took her over and settled her on the bed. He covered her and turned off the light.

She drifted off. He took the couch.

What a day was his last thought before he, too, fell asleep.

CHAPTER 47

The McCracken home resembled an estate. The developer had designed and built it himself. He'd spared no expense. The main house ran 7,000 square feet, of which the master bedroom was 2,000. With five bedrooms, a den, an office, and assorted other rooms, it was arguably the nicest home in San E. The grounds were landscaped to perfection with several water features both front and back. The swimming pool was of artistic design and fed by a fifteen-foot-high overhanging waterfall.

But the beauty of the place was of no importance on this night. McCracken sat in his office surrounded by a library of informational references as well as a world class collection of first editions. He was not smiling. His son, Mark, had called him earlier and demanded, actually demanded, a meeting.

As the clock struck eight, the younger McCracken arrived spot on time. He walked in to find his father seated at his elaborately carved desk, pushing some papers around in a seemingly random and unfocused manner.

The son strode up to the desk and stopped as would an Army private reporting for duty. But it was not he who would take orders, it was he who would deliver the momentous reprimand.

"Dad, I heard," said the boy. "I heard what you said to Sallie in her office."

"I don't know what you are talking about, Son," said the father, feigning innocence. "The mayor and I always speak in confidence. The door is always closed. It is the way she wants things. It's the private side of her public face. No one is ever in the room, and we never raise our voices. If you have heard something from someone about one of our conversations, I assure you that the person either is mistaken or is, in some way, trying to hurt the mayor. People in high places attract that kind of thing."

"Not this time, Dad. The easy explanation won't make this go away. I heard the conversation myself."

"I don't know what you thought you heard, but our conversations are always on the up and up." The father looked plaintively at his son. He could talk his way out of this, his son would go away, and then Mr. John McCracken, ruler of a small empire, could get on to reaming Beener's ass with respect to the Han situation. He expected Beener shortly, so he, regrettably, would give his son the bum's rush.

"I know about the development on the bluffs. I know what you have planned. I know about the Hans," said the son. "I was sitting outside the mayor's office, spelling Willie for a bathroom break. Apparently, Willie likes to listen—the intercom light was on. So, I listened."

The warm expression faded from McCracken's face. It gave way to a pallor that belied any further claims of innocence. "Son, I have to do things sometimes that go against all the things your grandparents taught me as a child. I feel I have to stretch the boundaries to get us where we need to be. This beautiful home is a monument to what I have accomplished. Had I not bent some rules, we would still be living in a dirty, white stucco, post-war house on the outskirts of San Diego. Look at this. Here we are minutes from the ocean. People here respect us. I've had to bend some rules, Son." It was his way of asking forgiveness.

"Dad. Sending that man to burn out the Hans was an absolutely horrid thing to do. You committed through that man, Beener, a major crime. A felony that can send you to prison. Dad, you've given up all you have worked for to end up in a six-by-eight steel cage. That is what you've done."

With his son close to tears, McCracken leaned back in his chair and could only sigh. After a couple of minutes, he spoke again. "I know this all looks bad. I guess I really didn't want the Hans to lose everything. I know I didn't want them nearly to be killed. I... I just have gotten into a mode where I can't help but bend principles and rules and even the law to have what I want. It has become an obsession to take all I can get. But it can be okay," he said, as if having a sudden revelation. "No one knows. I can make this right somehow. I can send Beener packing a long way from here. Maybe I could turn him in somehow."

Neither father nor son noticed the person who stepped into the doorway. "The only one here who can cause a problem is Little Lord Fauntleroy McCracken. Say good night, kid," Beener said as he pulled a silenced .45 caliber FN Tactical pistol from behind his back.

McCracken yelled, "Duck!" to his son as he swept his hand under his desk to grab the loaded Walther .380 PPK/S he'd bought for his wife.

Things went down quickly.

The son fell to the floor.

Beener saw the automatic in McCracken's hand. He turned his attention to the old man and fired.

The bullet, a fragmentation type that expended all of its energy when it struck something, hit McCracken in the right chest. The slug immediately split into pieces, destroying his right lung. Other pieces caromed off of his ribs and struck his heart.

McCracken managed to fire a single shot at Beener. It struck the paid goon in the forehead, killing him instantly.

The body's thud to the floor punctuated the deadly interchange.

McCracken knew his wound would prove fatal. He quickly scribbled some things down on a desk pad and signed his name.

In a way, that was justice, he supposed. As his son rushed to his side, he said, "I love you. I'm sorry. I love…"

Mark McCracken cradled his father's head. Ironically, the man's final act had been unselfish.

CHAPTER 48

Kimbel awoke several hours later and looked over for Susanna. Another disappearing act. He'd have to talk to her about that.

Just then, as if on cue, the door swung open. And there, in full glory and quite healthy, stood Susanna. Kimbel noticed a change of clothes, hair styled, and a smile on her full lips. His first thought: she must've gone insane. Or, she had a gun and planned to do them both in. The latter seemed most appropriate under the circumstances.

She lifted her forearm as to be conspicuous, and glanced purposefully at her watch. "Ah," she said. "The time for self pity has just passed. The time for revenge is nigh," she added, affecting a genuinely passable British accent. "C'mon, Mr. Happy Face, I have with me the perfect antidote for your blues. Please do take a seat at the table."

Kimbel, bewildered, sauntered over to the table and sat himself down.

Susanna then went outside and returned with a carryall sporting two very large cups of Starbucks. After depositing them on the table, she started unbuttoning her blood-red blouse.

Still in shock, Kimbel decided the Starbucks was a good idea. As he began to sip the scalding hot brew, he watched Susanna extract a folder from under the blouse. With that, she refastened the bottom buttons, although resorting to slow motion for effect.

"So. With the idea of getting laid first thing out of your head, you are probably wondering what you get for second place. A story. More specifically, an opinion piece to end all opinion pieces. You do go on and on with the sex thing, by the way. After a good couple of hours of sleep, I sat up with a start. I am Ms. Marketing as far as the *Observer* is concerned, and Ms. Marketing has all the chops to make this work. It will save both of our sorry asses—I need your help." She visually examined him for signs of life.

He was still practicing his *trying to see, but only able to stare* look.

She continued. "We have between us all that is necessary to drop the mother of all bombs on good old City Hall. With your Dexter Freehand editorials, we are aided in that you have already dropped bombs one, two, and three. The effort we are talking about here will be your fourth ... and last."

"Get me the yellow pages, please. I'm sure there is a copy in the Gideons' drawer. Select one of the numbers under the heading Psychiatrists. Make the call, and turn yourself in." He still could not muster a smile.

"If you don't shut up and listen, the only Yellow Pages you are going to get will be rolled up and inserted, by me, in suppository form."

Another sip of coffee, and he emitted a weak smile.

She sat down next to him. "What I have made is a list of our greatest strengths. And a second list ... of our ammunition. You with me? Nod."

He nodded.

"You can write like no one I have seen. I know what you did in Washington, or Fort Meade, or wherever else wasn't good for the enemies of this fine country. Who knows, maybe your job was to word them to death. In any event, my talents are in understanding the desired effect, knowing the target demographics, and in getting the desired response from them. Together, we can produce this quickly and effectively. We still need one other set of hands, and I have taken the liberty to make that call."

Kimbel attempted to speak, but Susanna would not relent.

"What we have for ammo are the following: 1) The public is already warmed up to this, 2) The new news is that there was a mini war at the McCrackens estate last night, and 3) we have the mayor for no less than three high crimes and misdemeanors. Ta-da," as she sang her way out of the thought.

"Alright," Kimbel jumped in. "My turn. What's wrong with number one is that the citizens were all warmed up by my articles. If my secret identity ever becomes public, the townspeople will want to take me to the beach as the tide comes in and bury me with only my head protruding. Let the waves do the work while they roast weenies and marshmallows. Second, I don't know what in the world you are talking about with respect to the McCrackens. It's probably irrelevant, anyway. Third and last, I can't even think of three high crimes and misdemeanors. So, unless I'm missing something…" he trailed off.

"Ah, but you are. Leave the crowd to me. I understand crowd dynamics. I also understand the power of three separate inert parts being brought together with explosive effect. Trust me, we've got it. That's number one. Number two is going to take some explaining."

She related how the police call had come in the early hours that there had been shots fired at the McCracken residence. She told him how the Police Chief said it all went down, and that the senior McCracken and his henchman were down hard. That meant dead.

"The son witnessed it all, and handed the investigating officer a note that his father had given him. In the terse note, McCracken laid out what Beener had done to the Hans home, and he described the symbiotic relationship he and the mayor had maintained for some time. *Everyone wins but the people.* That's what the note said."

"Wait," Kimbel interrupted. "You said something about McCracken having a son." He inflected it as more a question than a statement.

"This you're gonna love. I promise you," she said with a smile. "John McCracken did have a teenage son. The son was born 19 years ago to an unwed mother. Unwed because John did not want the obligation. Later, he felt guilty about walking away from his responsibility and got the young man a job. Here's the good part. He arranged an internship for him at City Hall." She gazed at Kimbel for the effect of the revelation. None. "Oh, I forgot the detail. His son's name is Mark."

His head spun.

"Mark was the name—the given name—of the McCracken representative who came to the Han's place, offering a deal! I threw him out!"

Kimbel was obviously shocked. "Holy Jesus!" he exclaimed. "I see what you mean! The mayor took the son in as an intern in partial payment for services rendered! What else?"

"Relax. You're smelling blood. The note continued. Big John admitted in his homicide note that our precious Mayor Sallie gave him the go ahead on pressuring your friends, the Hans. But wait, there's more." She was having fun now. "The third and final item is the *pièce de résistance*."

When she told him, he knew he was ready to lock and load. He knew that he was not yet done in and what he had to do. And, by God's good grace, he would pick up the ball and carry it until he either crossed the goal line or was stone cold dead.

It was then that the door opened, once again revealing someone that Kimbel least expected to see. He put that someone together with the person he knew who called her in, and could only shake his head. It looked like his story would enjoy a first class proofreader.

Luisa.

CHAPTER 49

It was after seven. The sun had succumbed to a moonless shroud of black outside. Mayor Sallie Goddard walked through the dimly lighted anteroom where Willie usually sat, but Sallie's major domo was long gone.

As she walked without much purpose into her office, she noticed that it was dark save for her desk lamp casting a bright light. The dim glow it produced elsewhere provided a surround of darkness. She sat down and breathed aloud, "A moment finally just for me."

She caught movement near the door and looked up. Surprised when a man stepped out of the darkness and into the low light, she knew his identity even before his features became clear. Her own personal grim reaper. She felt a shiver. And then he spoke.

"It is over, Mayor. I have found and connected all of the dots."

Her instincts jumped to the fore, even though her reservoir of personal strength was sapped. "Kimbel Stones, you probably couldn't find a dot with both hands. You couldn't connect several of them if I showed you how. You're a Washington, D.C. type, who thinks he can come into someone's town and push them around. It's the FFA agency that We The People seldom notice, but oversees all. Federal Fucking Arrogance. Well, I've got some serious news. I'm still in charge here, so you can take your dots and connections with you when you leave."

As much as Kimbel wanted to see her bleed, he just wanted to take her down and get the whole thing over. He wanted the Hans safe. That's all. Sallie was dead mayor walking, and he just wanted it done.

"I've got you for fronting zone changes for McCracken. I've got McCracken for bribery and for suborning felony crimes against the Hans. Here's the proof," he said as he tossed a small folder on her desk.

The mayor leafed through the pages of his evidence. There was little doubt it would connect her to the attacks on the Hans. She did not know his resources, but he clearly could produce a witness that put her and the developer together as conspirators.

Kimbel felt he needed item number three from his previous session with Susanna and Luisa. "There is, of course, additional information that you and a seventeen-year-old recently frolicked with sexual abandon on Santa Catalina Island. If you want to play this out, I can go there."

Sallie winced at the age number. She had not even thought to ask. That was worth some serious time in the slammer even if charges of collusion to commit murder did not stick.

"People always want something, Mr. Stones. What is your pleasure?" she said rhetorically, while only able to muster a faint *I give up* smile. She went on. "I thought I was on a rocket ship to the big time. Not only did I miss the liftoff, but it appears that the wash of the rocket's flame, as the ship left without me, has caught me on fire."

Kimbel listened without sympathy. He really wanted to terminate her with an extreme of prejudice, but that resolution would not go far enough.

It was time. Stones had the intel he'd received from the McCracken son. Recordings of the sounds of Sallie Goddard. Some, damning conversations. Others, sex—the activities on the offshore island of Catalina bought and paid for by the senior McCracken. It was clear from the latter that Sallie favored the fifteenth letter of the alphabet when bedding the young men.

Several of the conversations had her referring to Willie Sample, outside of his presence, as *that darling little faggot*. Politically incorrect for a Democrat. Stones played them all.

The mayor listened.

"This is California, Ms. Goddard. Your party will disown you."

"I've survived a lot worse. And the party? They'll blame the Russians."

"Then there's McCracken. Being implicated by this …" He cued the recording, and pressed *Play*.

Stones watched her listen.

He let it finish.

"I'd say—and a jury would say—attempted murder on the Hans. Two counts."

For the first time, desperation showed on Sallie Goddard's face. "We had to escalate until they caved. McCracken kept me in office. I had no choice."

"These recordings demonstrate that you were aware and cooperated."

An epiphany struck the mayor. A new tack. "You can't prove that's my voice."

Stones touched the screen, then tossed the tablet computer on the mayor's desk.

"It's called Voice Pattern Recognition. Those are the graphs from the McCracken recordings. I'll press *Compare* to the sample that I just took." He reached down and touched the screen button.

Her jaw dropped. Any further, and it would have hurt. She followed his eyes to the screen.

MATCH, it said.

ONE HUNDRED PERCENT.

Stones glanced up.

"That was the final piece."

"Piece of what?"

"Of GSM, Sallie. Game-Set-Match."

Mayor Sallie Goddard crossed her arms on her desk, then dropped her head on top.

Stones walked the room stopping before a gold-framed painting. A portrait.

"Margaret Goddard," he read from a brass plaque. "Your mother. You look just like her."

New sounds began to emanate from the desk. Sad sounds. Pained sounds.

Stones, who'd once considered himself a compassionate man, continued, this time in a softer tone. "Your last name suggests you never married. The ring on your finger suggests you are. Perhaps you returned to your maiden name after a failed relationship. The ring you still wear suggests that it was he who called it quits."

He watched as the words and their meaning sank into her core. The degree to which he despised her quickly deflected a fleeting pang of guilt.

Like his previous employer, he became just an observer of the broken woman.

Three discernable words escaped muffled sobs.

"Who are you?"

Several silent moments passed.

"You realize by now that I will dictate terms?" he asked rhetorically. "It will go down like this." He proceeded to lay out the terms.

Even in her much weakened state, her head jerked up but her jaw stayed down. She started shaking her head, but Kimbel's eyes would not negotiate.

"It … it can't be done. No amount of pedestrian ingrates can make that happen. There's the City Charter. There's state law. There's …"

Her voice, strong at the start, just tapered off to silence. "Fuck," was all she could say.

Just as the mayor was trying to catch her breath and regain control, another figure stepped out of the blackness to her left. She looked up to see a man dressed in black costume, the whiteness of a starched collar nearly matching the man's pale visage.

Sallie observed the priest even as she spoke to Kimbel, "I like it. My executioner has thought to bring along a fucking priest for Last Rites."

She could not take her eyes off him. There was something...

Then, he spoke with a softness that is the purview of the religiously indentured. "Sallie."

She stared bewildered. Then agape. "Omigod!" she gasped. "Oh, my fucking God!" Her expression simultaneously revealed terror and relief. "You... you went to prison. How could... omigod!"

It was too much. Sallie grabbed her face in her hands and began to shake and to sob. All self-control departed.

Kimbel gave her ten minutes to recover, then set some papers before her. She signed them. Triplicate. When she'd finished, she laid her head down on her arms.

All Kimbel heard was her muffled, favorite obscenity.

He picked up the papers and walked out. He had what he'd come for, while Sallie ran full speed into the very Karma she'd created.

As he walked through the door, he barely heard her voice in the background.

"Dad."

CHAPTER 50

The minister put his arm around his daughter as she stood, and he helped her from the room.

Now alone, Kimbel stepped out from the ante-room shadows, re-entered the office, and took the seat the mayor had just vacated.

Something caught his eye. In the corner. To the left of her desk lamp.

As focused as he'd been, he hadn't seen it before.

There it sat.

Next to a full glass of water.

Stones was certain that rat poison did not require water in order to prevent stomach upset.

Better worry about the convulsions, the vomiting, and death.

And the brand?

A well-known warehouse store chain that sold items only in large quantities.

Stones imagined a rat plague. Then, he considered the rats in City Hall. And those like McCracken, who'd fed them.

The unanswered question: had she seen the inevitable coming?

With the bottle's safety seal still in place, it was likely the mayor was just plain gone.

He rifled the drawers to find a half-filled box of .38 Special cartridges. No gun, and nothing else of interest other than a four-page user guide for a Smith & Wesson snub nose.

Stones wondered. Why didn't she use it? Maybe she realized that all good things come to an end. Maybe she just decided to move on.

At that moment and for the first time, reality caught up with him.

"I'm in charge here," he said out loud. "I'm truly in charge. Holy crap!"

He laughed an easy laugh. Then, a slow breath, and exhale.

With that, he took a moment to reflect.

In a short time, one Kimbel Stones had invaded the eastern-most Russian territory, stolen a critical intelligence artifact, survived an epic escape through a Siberian blizzard, been rescued from certain death by a CIA operative known as Magic Man, recovered just in time to rescue his adoptive parents from a corrupt mayor and her developer partner-in-crime, survived a track-down and capture for nefarious purposes by the Russian blonde, and finalized the whole deal by succeeding the displaced mayor. His only question ... what to do for an encore?

His moment of peace terminated abruptly.

Wrong phone. And worse, the wrong ring.

"Yes?"

The deep, processed voice provided, "E 2 Q. Say again, E 2 Q."

Stones entered the Crypto Index to select the necessary decryption algorithm. He touched the PROCEED button on the screen.

The voice continued. "Reference 1227B regarding Codename: Magic Man unmask request. Clearance and need-to-know verified. Black ops solo, in-the-cold, GS-19 Lethality Technician Level 5. Danger index: ten of ten."

Stones stared transfixed at the screen.

The connection remained alive…

"Uh!" exuded the processed voice. "*Uhhhhhh!*"

His breath caught in his throat.

With the voice transform in place, he couldn't indentify who'd been talking, tell who apparently was being attacked, or who'd just been killed.

Quick, he stabbed the phone with his finger.

Again.

Again.

Until the device waxed quiescent.

His breathing accelerated toward a full-on panic response.

He grabbed the glass of water on the mayor's desk, still filled with ice, still cold.

He pressed it hard near the carotid sinus to the right of his windpipe.

Ten, fifteen, twenty seconds.

He calmed.

"What was that?" He exhaled. "What the hell was that?"

The phone sprang back to life.

The voice, "Got your attention?"

Stones, shaken, nodded affirmation.

"Per request. Codename Magic Man. Not NSA. CIA. Operative Crayle… Magus Crayle. I say again. Crayle… Magus Crayle."

This time, the phone turned itself off.

Stones, mouth hanging open, set it on the desk as smoke began to pour out.

Crayle.

On Little Diomede.

The man who'd saved his life.

CHAPTER 51

The atmospheric conditions within the Sacramento, California Governor's Mansion mirrored those of the pounding, gale-blown rains outside. The skies mid-day were severely dark and the torrential downpour darkened the moods of both men. Their political careers were now on a course south, both figuratively and literally.

The present goings on in the small coastal town called San Ernestino added to other political losses escalating across recent years. Their party's death grip on the state's voters trended to full limp.

The thin one pulled his head from his hands, and glanced across at the chubby one.

"This populism thing has got to stop. All our side deals start going south as soon as any old John Smith gets popular *and* elected."

"Look, Chub. We wanted it gone and business back to usual a couple of election cycles ago. Didn't happen."

"You need to stop referencing my Garfield-like appearance and call me by my given name."

"When I took the oath, I promised to tell the truth, the whole truth, and nothing but the truth." He paused for a smirk. "Sorry. Go ahead."

"Yeah, Spindle-fump."

The portly member of the inseparable pair sat back. As Lieutenant Governor, he'd been boosted to the state hot seat upon a mob-induced death of his former boss, the governor. The public, outraged by the exposed actions of his predecessor—and his party—demanded that a non-party substitute be found for the job. A quirk in the state constitution allowed for such a move. Back on point, he continued.

"It's not just California. It's across the nation. These non-partisan guys get elected and, instead of falling flat on their faces, succeed. They've done government better and cheaper."

"One, I prefer Slim. Two, and far more important, we have to deal with this issue right now. This Stones down south is way popular."

"Take him down."

"So, we get a hit man?"

"Wait, I'll check my contact list," the thin one said. "Nope. No hit men. Let's just paint him as a racist… or a misogynist."

"That your fancy word begins with 'miso' is making me hungry."

"Seriously?"

"Those dirty trick techniques have worn thin with the public. The folks've wised up. Hey, wait a minute." Chub's eyes became narrow slits. "You tilt your chin like that and produce that phony thin smile when you're digging in. So, that's it then, Slim. A hit man?"

"Better than that. Now that Kimbel Stones performed all the heavy lifting, we make him one of us."

Chub started to talk, but stopped. Then laughed a triple-chin laugh before reaching over and clapping his hand onto the other man's shoulder. "That's exceptional. Up there with *The Contract With America* as a coup, my friend."

"Thanks. We're not friends, I remind you. Politicians don't have friends. Self-interests up to the point of clinical narcissism. Partners in crime. And the rest. Not friends."

He examined the ceiling as if checking for listening devices.

"Here it is. This Stones is a shoe-in ... and we pull the strings."

"Out of sight of the audience."

Slim gleamed. "We become the Marionette Party."

The other man poured from a crystal decanter of home-made peppermint Schnapps left behind by a Republican. They drank a toast.

"Wait. What do we know about this guy? He just shows up one day, goes to work at the local newspaper, and unseats our woman, who had a lock on the mayor's office. Where'd he come from? Who'd he work for?"

"Would you like that assignment as homework? For tomorrow?"

"Tomorrow? It'd take longer than that."

"We don't have longer than that."

"So, who talks to the guy?"

"That's your homework." He produced a moist hand. "Shake."

They did, then lifted their glasses once more.

"Kimbel Stones. Here's to Governor Stones."

They moved off to the executive washroom. With the lid still up from the last time, they took positions on each side of the commode, and began their business.

"It just occurred to me there might be a fly in this particular ointment, Slim."

"My ideas are picture perfect."

"Like Mission Accomplished?"

"Go."

"Try this out. A non-party governor would bring in his own people. They'd discover all the dirty tricks of ours that make Tricky Dick Nixon look like integrity personified. Graft, sweetheart deals, kickbacks, pay-to-play deals ... we've done it all. We handed out rose-colored glasses to the people and, in their eyes, could do no wrong."

"The chickens, as they say, will be coming home to crap all over us if we don't get this right."

"If we could only send this character, Stones, somewhere else."

"Yeah, out of state."

The door burst open. The administrative assistant, a very cool brunette, ran into the office, across the floor, and stopped at the bathroom opening.

The two men, three-quarters drunk, didn't even look around.

"Sorry, Gladys. The stool's full," Chub said, paraphrasing a line from Top Gun.

They both laughed, nearly wetting themselves, and each other.

Gladys Prandy, who'd seen far worse in the governor's office, delivered her message unaffected.

"Crisis time, gentlemen. The V.P. of the entire U.S. of A.? He's dead. Wife ran him over. One of you'll have to step up a notch."

"Step up?" Slim shook his head. Both of them. "We're not going to that hellhole."

"No-oh-no" said Chub. "Sorry about the V.P., but…"

They stopped in process. They looked at one another.

"Kimble Stones!" Chub cried.

"Manna from heaven," said Slim.

The two laughed so hard that, this time, they did get each other wet.

The brunette, seeing it coming, managed to dodge the line of fire.

Chub and Slim slapped a high-five—with the wrong hands—and cried out in unison.

"Kimble Stones!"

CHAPTER 52

The scene at San Ernestino's City Hall resembled anything but normal. It closely matched the circumstances of Kimbel Stones' unlikely ascent to head of the local government.

Managing Editor Treadwell had assured that the population rolls and the paper's subscriber list were merged with respect to mailed invitations. He'd gone further with a full front page advertisement that bade everyone welcome as well. The banner headline read,

HELL, YEAH! IT'S ABOUT TIME!

The former Mayor Goddard, her entire staff, and all of their belongings were gone. It resembled the indoor version of a ghost town with one exception. The sole semblance of a transition team, Goddard lieutenant Willie Sample, greeted the crowd with vintage 2002 Louis Roederer Cristal champagne complemented with French Bakery hors d'oeuvres. It was time to honor the victory.

The celebration party included everyone from the Observer, as well as an extensive cross-section of the town's populace. Susanna even coaxed the city's most famous resident—the studio-tanned, Oscar-winning actress, Erin Pleshette—from the comforts of her lavish home.

Kimbel also made sure the invitation included the Hans. After all, they had taken the brunt of the Mayor Goddard and John McCracken onslaught. Bettie was still confined to a wheel chair, but Kimbel called Quentin up to the podium to a round of applause. His long-time friend and substitute father had stood up strong for the town, something no-one would ever forget.

The new mayor bestowed on him the newly-minted Order of San Ernestino. Quentin accepted graciously. Susanna appeared, dressed like the marketing hotshot that she was. Luisa was also there, but all the men gave her a little room. It was as if they might get too close and succumb to weakness.

The celebration contained all the glitz of the olden days. Kimbel stood on a platform, smiling his best mayoral smile, and everyone applauded the fine job he'd done. After the swearing in by a local judge, it was time to anoint Kimbel with the medallion of office.

The medallion itself had been crafted locally in the 1950's. And, although it appeared to be made of gold, everyone suspected it to be something less. Normally, the outgoing mayor performed the transfer of power ceremony by removing the medallion and personally placing it on the new mayor. The situation at San E did not allow for tradition since Sallie Goddard was nowhere to be found. Apparently, she had given an old realtor friend the listing for her place, and told him to forward the proceeds to her dad's parish. She then took what she could carry in her town-bought luggage and flew the coop.

As vice mayor, a tell-it-like-it-is title if there ever was one, Willie stood in for Sallie and did a fine job. He was so used to it, he almost gave Kimbel a big kiss on the cheek. He caught himself just before he made contact, then decided to leave the cheek kissing to the French.

Everyone quaffed champagne, laughed, and story-told until late in the afternoon. After that, they went their separate ways. As the editor Silas Treadwell departed, he noticed Kimbel seated in the mayor's chair, gazing off into space and wondering what could possibly come next.

The sun rose the next day as it always did. Life in San E continued on. Editor Treadwell continued on with his work. He had to find a new political reporter.

And when the new sun set, it produced a resplendent red sky that none of the townspeople would ever forget.

In his office, Silas Treadwell mused that Mayor Stones had a good ring to it. It was a strong name, as his mother would have said.

For a moment, he sat back and wondered what he had just done. What he had set in motion. What might become of the enigmatic man from back East.

With that, the editor glanced over at the coffee pot and remembered the very first day.

Yeah, a good hire.

EPILOGUE

It was just sixty days after the new mayor took office in San Ernestino that, far away in Washington, D.C., the White House Chief-Of-Staff burst into the Oval Office. The president dropped his very favorite food item, jerked back in his chair, and started to climb under his desk.

He stopped when he saw the tears flowing down the face of his closest advisor.

The man tended toward the effusive. The nation's chief executive returned to his previous posture to finish his afternoon snack.

"You haven't heard?" the COS wailed.

"Heard what?"

"There's been an assassination!"

"What?"

The COS had caught his boss in mid-bite. He readied for the Heimlich maneuver.

"Not necessary," the man behind the desk choked out. "Who?"

"The president!"

"I'm the president—I'm just fine." He bit into the final chipotle-lime shrimp.

"Not you! The golfing one!"

"You're crazy. He's playing golf in Ghana."

The COS punched a code into a remote control.

George Washington's portrait rotated out, revealing a high-definition screen.

Another button powered on the television.

"Oh, my God!" the president exclaimed. "Terrorists!"

The Chief-Of-Staff gulped and panted until he regained a semblance of control. "It's worse. Real worse. They've taken out all the top names in that administration—the whole crew. Today."

"But those people have security guards."

"He'd gotten rid of their firearms in support of gun control legislation."

"That wasn't supposed to include us."

"Six of them ... guards ... all down hard."

The president began to hyperventilate.

"Are we in lockdown?"

"Not at this point. It's a group."

"Foreign terrorists?"

"Domestic. Call themselves Payback."

In the unlikeliest of moments, the consummate politician in the room scored an epiphany. "It's the James Earl Ray thing. Déjà vu. With all due respect for the dead, we can take this to the election. Ba-da-bing! We win."

The COS shook his head. "Not so. Payback is black. Their motto: Enough's enough."

"That's all we need. Black Republican fanatics."

"Wrong again, Sir. They call themselves centrists. Constitutional."

"They took out six guarded individuals. Suddenly, I don't feel safe."

"They've taken a page from Al Qaeda. They'll die for their cause."

"Could this sort of notion—to die for a cause—be duplicated?"

"Another unit has formed in Alaska. They want your head."

"Any more wonderful news?"

"There's a guy in California. He's taken over a town as mayor."

"Payback?"

"In the meaning of the word, yes. But, so far, no links established to the terrorists."

"So what. If I haven't heard of him, he's not politically interesting."

"They said that about a junior senator from Illinois."

"Alright. Once my personal safety has been assured, form a covert unit and see that this player isn't allowed to play. We've done this before. Hopefully, some of those operatives are still alive."

"Yes, Sir. Uh, what'll I tell them to do with the corpse … after?"

The president, still on edge, laughed. "Lay it out in a federal park. We've done that before, too."

"There might be a small problem."

"No problem too large for the president."

"He's the one who brought out the Diomede intel."

"Oh?"

"Kimbel Stones."

The president grabbed at his chest. He lunged for his heart pills.

• • •

The next day's editorial page posted an editorial … by the editor. Seldom did he feel the need to write since San E was, in normal times, as sleepy a town as existed. Here's what it said.

> *For once, I'm going to let myself ramble a bit. Here goes.*
>
> *This is where we are a short few months after Kimbel R. Stones arrived in our otherwise tranquil town. The protests died down immediately when he took over and made it clear that he could, without any interference, turn things around in short order. And he did.*

Without a council to deal with, he passed an ordnance banning gangs. After all, he reasoned, a gang is defined to be people who form an organization for the purpose of committing crimes. All known gang members were identified, rounded up by Chief Connor and crew, and the crime rate plummeted. Citizens enjoyed no longer being fearful of venturing out after dark, even in their nice neighborhoods. The remaining criminals did not like the new San E and moved elsewhere, mostly upstate to San Francisco.

Police Chief Connor and his men were ecstatic. The daily risk from crime had been reduced by 87%. He admitted that this was the first time in his career that a town had stood firmly behind law enforcement. He also knew he would have no trouble filling vacancies, and pay would become a non-issue.

The improvements were so many and so quick, the nearby two communities demanded the same. Their political leaders were forced to come to Kimbel for help. By the time they left, San Ernestino had annexed Ventria and Runon Beach into a larger and more powerful community that was renamed San Ernesto—no longer Little Ernie. I would like to take credit for the new name, but credit actually belongs to senior and sole reporter, Tram Nguyen.

Neither John McCracken nor his hit man, Beener Jackman, could be charged with their crimes since they were both dead. The senior McCracken penned a note prior to the ending of his life. In his note, he stated that the hit man had threatened to kill his son and so he had shot the man to death. He also said that his son had proved more honorable than he, and that it was because of his unworthiness as a father that he had considered taking his own life. He hoped his son would be honored for his courage.

Former Mayor Sallie Goddard was nowhere to be found. Rumor was that she had packed up and headed for the great northwest. If she had gone to ground in all of that space, it would be difficult tracking her down to face charges. A document mailed to the Observer detailed all of the conversations overheard in the mayor's office. I had an expert perform an analysis, and the handwriting was matched to a Mark McCracken sample. The new mayor did issue a proclamation heralding the youngster's sense of honor and the price he'd been willing to pay.

Then there was the Breaking News. Park rangers found the bodies of two men, one large and one thin, up north on a beach next to a lake. Autopsies reported that they'd been fatally shot with .38 caliber rounds, one each. It was not interesting until they were identified. And, then the rangers spotted the body of a woman washing against the shore fifty yards away.

First take, by the local sheriff, was that one Sallie Goddard had been visited by men from the California governor's office. She'd shot them dead. It appeared that she then walked out into the water, and drowned.

Too bad. The men had tracked her down in order to offer her the vacant governor's position. Definitely, too bad.

Susanna Thomson was forgiven by Kimbel. I did keep her on and she responded by not only increasing circulation within the borders of old San E, but she lit out into the new suburbs of Ventria and Runon Beach and nearly tripled the Observer's ad space. Shoot, we added so many pages, I hired more reporters and an assistant proofreader/copy boy. Well, actually it was a copy girl. I didn't mean to be sexist, it was just important that the new employee actually could get some meaningful work done.

And the Hans. They recovered nicely and started trying to put their lives back in order. Part of the liquidation of McCracken Development paid for a rebuild of the old home, brought up to modern specifications. Mark McCracken inherited the company, and he made sure the Hans got even more than they had before. There was none of the usual corner cutting on building codes, and he personally dropped by to present them with a bill with a zero balance. In a final act, he presented them with a deed to the rest of the bluff property that his father had acquired.

The interior had to be refurnished, but Misses Han had saved all of the photographs she had of their home in a safe deposit box. Having them and her husband meant everything to her. They sent a package containing a one gallon jar of native Korean Kimchee to San Ernesto's new mayor, along with a card thanking him for all he had done. In return, he sent them a professionally-restored, 1960, light blue, Route 66 Corvette.

The Observer and its editor, me, achieved new life. What had occurred excited my sorry ass about future prospects.

Of course, Mayor Stones will some day move on and have to be replaced, but even with his new title and position, he still allows Editor Silas Treadwell, me, to call him Kimbel and, oh… wait… there goes Luisa…

–30–

ABOUT THE AUTHOR

Thriller writer Dennis Bowen has researched his novels in more than 60 countries. Realism and spice infuse his stories, thus reflecting his wartime service and his background in the defense and intelligence communities. One of his readers accurately observed, "Bowen knows his stuff."

STONES is the first novel in Bowen's new Backstory Files Series. It provides a heart stopping yet intriguing background for one of the primary characters in his bestselling International Thriller Series, currently at five books. Included are ***The Water Diamonds (1)***, ***The Blackstone Perfection (2)***, ***The Crystal Seduction (3)***, ***The Redrock Quarantine (4)***, and ***The Final Masquerade (5)***.

When not traveling the globe for inspiration and intel for his stories, Dennis Bowen resides on the Southern California coast.

Twitter: http://www.twitter.com/DBowenThrillers/
Facebook: http://www.facebook.com/DennisBowenThrillers
Website: http://www.dennisbowen.com/

THE VIRTUE TRANSITION

BOOK 6: INTERNATIONAL THRILLER SERIES

Available: Fall 2018

CHAPTER 1

"I met someone."

The man seated across from the stoic woman said nothing. Like her, he stared down at the paint-chipped and splintered picnic table.

That three little words could cause so much damage was unknown to them. Their last three little words had been "I love you" spoken at their wedding.

Silence followed by more silence.

She stood and turned, exhaling, depleted.

She watched the nearby lake as its waves lapped at the water's edge, but heard nothing.

Even the birds in the eighty-foot pine tree not ten feet away waxed quiescent.

A distant buzz, probably teens playing with toy aircraft, penetrated the gloomy mood.

"It … it …"

"I want to hear," he whispered. "Tell me."

A gust blew past, tossing a loose paint chip to the ground. That covert team member, Lenny Lipschitz, had applied cheap paint over the original redwood as a gesture of friendship didn't matter.

To Hekka Crayle, the table symbolized their relationship. Once strong. Once steady. Now, coming apart. Unraveling.

"I need to know," said the man she'd grown to love. To fight alongside. To fight for.

"I can't, Magus … I … uh"

The percussion of the next moment stopped the discussion dead.

It nearly stopped *them* dead.

One of five armed drones had plowed into the tree, gusted there by the wind. There, to explode.

Crayle yanked Hekka's arm just in time. He rolled right.

Damaged, the tree shook, then emitted an explosive sound of its own.

Two seconds later, another loud crack. The tree leaned. The third crack was final.

The crashing pine missed the Crayles. Barely. It hit the log cabin dead on.

"*Micmac! Phoebe! They're inside!*"

They glanced back in the direction of the attack.

Two of the four armed drone escorts had splintered and fallen from the blast.

Switching to Plan B, the other two opened fire. Caliber .22 rounds arrayed inside their fuselages provided a barrage of deadly potential.

The Crayles fought to protect each other from the fusillade.

Inside the cabin, former SEAL/UDT veteran Micmac and current on-leave FBI Agent Phoebe had been working on a covert ops training video.

The explosion outside should have blown the sliding door and adjacent glass window into deathly shards. Bullet proof, bomb proof, they held strong. The roof, however, had not been strengthened to stop a huge, falling tree six feet in girth.

The two dove away from each other. An instinctive ploy such that one or the other might survive.

Having landed in the kitchen, Phoebe forced open the side door and skirted the cabin.

Pinned by the couch that had slammed the wall, Micmac heard his ops game continue unabated with its own gunfire and explosions.

The last thing he heard before passing out—two booming shots. He smiled. His world went dark.

Phoebe had limped alongside the cabin to its rear. She took in the drones fixated on Crayle and Hekka. Micmac had heard Phoebe's .45 caliber Glock speak.

FBI colleagues referred to her as Annie Oakley for her deadly accuracy.

Two shots. Two drones.

Offshore, a camouflage-dressed man fired up his boat's three Mercury outboards and sped off.

A similarly clad cohort flew a sixth drone, its video streaming into her Smartphone complete, into the waves. The diminutive woman smiled, threw her drone controller into the lake, and ducked out of sight.

Crayle would never forget the flag hanging from the craft's stern.

He rolled his head to the right. To where his pregnant wife had landed.

Gone.

Having slammed his head against the picnic bench, he fought for consciousness.

A light snow began, the season's first.

He begged a desperate pair of eyes for clarity instead of the fog.

No Hekka.

"Where ..." he gasped. "... where ..."

Fall 2018

THE VIRTUE TRANSITION

From International Thriller Writer
DENNIS BOWEN

www.ingramcontent.com/pod-product-compliance
Lightning Source LLC
Chambersburg PA
CBHW020610310726
48979CB00008B/1422/J